PRODIGAL

SON

ISBN: Softcover 978-1-5028-1437-1
eBook 978-1-3112-3323-3

This book was printed in the United States of America.

Rev. date: 10/16/2016

To Rolando –

for being a great sounding board and not being too put off
that his wife writes about pulling off a good murder.

Contents

PRODIGAL SON

Prologue

"Christ!" was the only word from Shuller. He stood dumbfounded in the street as his deputy rattled off what little detail they had. Danny knew better than to let Shuller inside, giving him a moment to recover. This one hit home, too close to home. She never hurt a soul. Shuller saw her just yesterday. It was the last thing he wanted to deal with. He had barely recovered from his last odd ball case. This made no sense. He had not seen this coming. Not to her.

"Her, of all people," the deputy sputtered. The statement caught Shuller off guard.

"Would there have been someone better?" Shuller barked. He took offense at the statement merely due to the fact he was having his own selfish thoughts about it. He realized he snapped at the officer but didn't apologize. Besides, it was the shock talking.

"Uh, no. No, of course not! But boss, you've got to admit, of all people, why her, why like that?" he asked, almost pleading.

"Yeah. Jesus!" Trying to comprehend, Shuller attempted to rationalize why, forget about the how. The *how* was much more gruesome to deal with at the moment. He listened to what Danny was saying, but it still sounded too unbelievable. His mind was on overload trying to process it all. *How could this happen, here, to her?* he wondered. This wasn't some crime-ridden city. This was Any Town, USA; a regular cookie cutter type of town. Things like *this* don't happen here.

"There was blood everywhere. We're hoping the freak left prints."

Shuller didn't respond. This bastard's prints being in the system would be too perfect. He knew deep down that it would not be that easy, not by a long shot.

PRODIGAL SON

Chapter One

Scuff, scuff, scuff.

Vivian shuffled around her vacant house doing her mundane chores. It was a preoccupation to keep her house immaculate. She spent most of her time these days dusting and casually rearranging her tchotchkes. The sexagenarian, adorned in her favorite housedress and slippers, systematically moved from room-to-room. She surveyed the décor, ensuring it remained visitor ready at all times.

Her home was her pride and joy. It was all she had left. There was nobody left for her to take care of; there was no one left to take care of her, either. Vivian and her husband Richard had decided long ago they were not the parenting type and never had any children of their own. They were single children of single children. As time marched on, they had less and less family to speak of overall. There were random and distant relatives scattered across the country. They had second cousins somewhere but lost touch in the years after their parents had passed. Several years back, time eventually took Richard as well.

Now it was just Vivian, her rheumatoid arthritis, and the house. Even when she and Richard had both occupied the residence, the sheer size swallowed them both. The home was three stories of Victorian wallpaper, elaborate window treatments, and forlorn area rugs that quite possibly had seen the best of their years decades ago. It was excessively massive for two people milling about, but the house was in Vivian's family for generations. That tradition apparently would end with her. With it just being Vivian and her collectibles, living in the house made even less sense than it had before.

Vivian broke from her chores and came to rest on the settee in the foyer. The two antiques creaked as they both settled in the silence of the hall. She felt older than her age given the arthritis. As she sat, her eyes traced along the walls, the edges of doorframes, and a sad smile crept to her face. The morning light streamed through the stained glass above the doorway. Specs of floating dust, early morning evidence of her cleaning efforts, caught by the light gently glided through the air. The faint *tick tick tick* echoed from the mantle clock in the sitting room. Vivian's thoughts and the ghosts of the past were her only companions. She sat with a tight-lipped smile and exhaled forcibly through her nose. She had already accomplished her daily chores, and it was only nine a.m.

Clank clank clank.

The sound of the doorknocker jolted Vivian from her quiet repose. She recovered and grappled for the upholstered handle of the settee in order to raise herself from the cushions. She shuffled herself to the inner door of the entranceway.

"Just a minute," she hollered to the large shadow through the frosted glass of her front door.

"Take your time, Viv," the shadow yelled back, hearing another clank of the knocker as he released it.

A smile came to her face rather quickly. Her pace quickened a bit despite the wish of the visitor. She hobbled to the front door. Grabbing the glass doorknob with her right hand to steady herself, she reached up and turned the deadbolt. She pulled back on the door.

"Well hello, dear," Vivian greeted her early morning visitor. Her face lit up as a large smile pushed aside her delicately wrinkled cheeks. She squinted as she looked up at her visitor the sun streamed into the foyer behind him.

"Well good morning, Viv. Figured you'd already be up and about, so I didn't bother with the bell," Shuller said. He had made it a point some time back to visit Vivian at least once a week.

"Well, that bell gave up the ghost a few weeks back, so good thing you used the knocker," she chuckled.

"Oh? Well, why didn't you tell me? I'll be by this weekend to fix it for you," Shuller said as he glanced down at the doorbell.

"That's kind of you dear, but don't trouble yourself," she smiled back at him.

While she wasn't the only senior citizen in town, she was the only one who had no family to speak of to check in on her. Shuller took it upon himself to be the one who checked on her routinely. She had her share of visitors, though, and she would get around town herself. Shuller, not unlike Vivian, was on his own, too. His drop-ins with Vivian for their morning tea were almost more for him than it was for her.

"I thought I'd come by for some tea," Shuller explained.

"Well of course, dear. You're a few weeks late now, aren't you?" she asked in jest as she shuffled aside for him to enter.

"Well, yes. Trust me, if I could have been by sooner, I would have," Shuller said as he crossed the threshold. He held his hand out in front of him as he took control of the front door. Vivian turned toward the kitchen as Shuller closed and locked up before following her down the hall.

Vivian had already made it to the kitchen in record speed. She had missed his visits while he was out of town. She sprung back to action, thrilled to be back to her routine. She took the kettle off the baker's rack and turned to the sink.

Shuller heard the water running before he ever made it to the kitchen. As he entered, he headed straight for the table. He knew better than to try to help her. She would only scold him as she had done in the past. Vivian had finished filling the kettle and dropped it onto the cast-iron grill of her gas stovetop. The familiar *click click, whoosh* of the gas stovetop coming to life was a welcomed sound. Vivian then took her seat at the table while they waited for the kettle whistle.

"So, glad to be home?" Vivian asked as she reached for the glass sugar bowl.

"You have no idea, Viv." Shuller sighed. "Trust me when I say I missed your Earl Grey more than you'll ever know."

"Read about that case in the papers. Poor girl." Vivian shook her head.

"Yeah, that was a strange one. But justice was done and all is as it should be," Shuller said. "I'm just glad Samantha wasn't nicked for something she didn't do." Shuller tried to avoid talking about the case. He knew his efforts would prove fruitless, as she would soon quiz him on every aspect she read in the papers. The Harrigan case still baffled him.

"Why would he let that happen to someone else, though? That's the part that made no sense to me," she questioned Shuller.

"You and me both, Viv. It made less sense to me, and I was there." Shuller sighed, avoiding Vivian's gaze. "How could a parent do that to a child they brought into this world? You're supposed to take care of your children, not leave them to fend for themselves," Shuller said, annoyed at the thought once again.

"Hmmm," Vivian uttered, dipping her head.

"I was concerned about you while I was gone," Shuller said, changing the subject. He noticed Vivian pursed her lips slightly but wasn't quite sure what to make of it. "I was worried you were going to be too lonely."

"Aw, you're a dear. You have better things to do than to worry about me. I'm just fine." She perked back up soothing his concerns instantly. "Danny took time to come by to check on me." She laughed. "Guess he figured it was part of your day job."

"I asked Danny to check on you while I was away. I just didn't plan to be gone as long as I was. Well, it may not be my job officially, but I wouldn't be doing my job if I didn't worry about everyone in town. I'm just finicky on who I call on to visit for tea." He smiled just as the faint whistle of the kettle diverted Vivian's attention. She staggered to her feet and clicked off the burner. Shuller grabbed two teacups from their hooks and their accompanying saucers and put them on the counter top by the stove. Vivian shot him a crooked eye. Shuller raised his hands in surrender and reclaimed his seat at the table.

Vivian reached for the canister on the counter and took out two tea bags. Each bag deposited in a cup, Vivian carried the cups to the kitchen table, balancing them over the saucers she had palmed under each cup. Shuller reached out for his cup and saucer. Vivian then placed hers down close to mismatched sugar bowl that was present on the table. The nerve-racking part was coming for Shuller. He had to sit and watch the sixty-seven-year-old, arthritis-ridden woman handle a kettle of boiling water. With both hands, she picked up the kettle and headed for the table. Despite his trepidations, Vivian had no difficulties pouring the steaming water into the two cups before placing the kettle to the stovetop and then returning to her seat at the table.

"What's next on the horizon?" Vivian asked as she eased her way onto the cushioned chair at the table. She removed her tea bag, giving it a good squeeze before depositing it on the saucer and started adding the first of two teaspoons of sugar.

"Oh, hopefully a lot of nothing," Shuller said as he dunked his tea bag. "I'm just enjoying being back home. Regular routine, that's what I hope the future has in store."

"Well, here's to the same old same old then," she said raising her cup.

"Here, here!"

The early summer sun warmed the air. Shuller left the company of Ms. Vivian Nash after a lengthy discussion of the Harrigan murder case. It was more detail and rehashing than he had wanted, but he had satisfied her rabid curiosity, as usual. He had conceded and filled her in on some of the details that weren't splashed all over the local papers. She hung on his every word as if he was one of her daily stories. Inwardly he didn't mind. He enjoyed spending time with her, and their many lengthy conversations. Over the years and many visits together, she had become somewhat of a surrogate mother to him. The way she had come to dote on him, she had all but adopted him. It was a connection to family. A connection they both had missed for so long.

PRODIGAL SON

Shuller strolled down the tree-lined sidewalk on his way to the station. Kids played in their front yards, newly released from school for summer break. The trees rustled in the wind above his head while the heels of his well-worn boots crunched against the thin layer of dirt that coated the concrete below. Sheets flapped in the breeze as they hung off someone's backyard line in the distance. *Ah, home.*

Shuller inhaled deeply. He was sure relief was scrawled across his face. While he was not far away working the Columbus Cove case, getting back home, to his life and routine, that was a warm feeling he embraced. He could not help but compare his current settings to that of the Cove. Despite the two towns being a several minutes apart by car, the differences between the two towns seemed like worlds apart. He hadn't realized just how much he missed tarmac and cement sidewalks. He thought he'd never finish dusting that town off him.

While he was anxious to come home, returning home did mean returning to an empty house. In that sense, he was much the same as Vivian. It was a passing thought every now and then. *Would I end up like that, frail and alone?* That's what made their visits more important to him than it may have ever been to her, but he'd never let her know. Perhaps someone would one day do that for him. That thought he kept to himself. He kept most anything personal close to the vest. He felt it safer to keep emotions in check and private, no matter who was involved. That came from years of conditioning from both personal lessons gleamed from heartache and years of police work combined.

Shuller turned up Parker Street. As soon as he rounded the corner, the smell of fresh baked bread enveloped him.

Must be just coming out of the oven, he thought. *Once the smell carries its way through the neighborhood, Sherry will be hard at work replenishing the supply.* Sherry, the bakery owner, waved from behind the counter at Shuller as he passed her large windows. The shadow of the painted window fell across the display case already stocked with various delights.

Shuller continued to amble his way down the street toward the station. He took his time as he was not due back to work until tomorrow. His backfill had one more day playing sheriff before Shuller had to resume his duties. Besides, he knew his secretary would give him an earful as soon as he got anywhere near his desk. Shuller could not help himself but to drop in to see the guys and get a read for anything he missed while he was away.

Before he even realized it, he was approaching the double doors of the station. He found himself smiling at the black antiqued lampposts topped with large white globes that flanked the entranceway. He turned to enter the building, his back to the families already sprawled out on sheets on the large grass park across the street from the station. He trotted up the three concrete steps and entered the station. Phones ringing, water cooler conversations in the distance, and the typical office commotion. He stood just past the doors taking in the normal scene with a grin. It was a few seconds or so before Shuller was noticed in the lobby.

"Hey there, boss! Almost didn't see ya there. You back today? Wasn't expecting you until tomorrow," called out the front desk clerk, Frank.

"Nah, you're right. I'm due back tomorrow officially. Just wanted to drop in and get caught up, see how the guys were doing, you know."

"You work-a-holic," Frank replied. "Think you'll be able to get past the bulldog? Don't think for one minute Susan isn't going to give you crap for coming in today."

"Oh, yeah. I know," Shuller sighed, pushing aside the half doors connected to the corner of the counter. The swinging doors barely stopped as she caught sight of him.

"Are you seriously here?" she snapped as he approached her desk. The station was alerted to Shuller's presence. He got the spattering of waves from fellow officers while others gave him a look of sympathy as they knew the tongue-lashing he was about to experience.

"Glad to see you, too, Suzie Q," Shuller said as he smiled.

"Humph. You have one more day before you have to be back at work. Go home and come back tomorrow," she said firmly, shooing him away with a wave of her hand.

"Wow, now I know you missed me, but try to contain your enthusiasm. You're embarrassing yourself," he chuckled. "I just got here and already getting the bum's rush out the front door."

"Uh, yes! You hardly ever take any time off. Now go," Susan said, "enjoy the day for crying out loud. Emails and paperwork can wait until tomorrow," she added, cutting off his attempted response. Shuller took a seat on the edge of her desk. Susan was not to be trifled with when she had her mind set.

"There is a time to work and a time to rest. Take your rest. Catch up on some TV or something. Go next door to Mitchell's and get yourself a haircut. Looks like it's grown a millimeter since your last buzz. It must be driving you mad." She flashed him a jovial smile.

"It *is* a bit untamed," he jested, rubbing his hand atop of his head. "Paperwork you say? Anything go on while I was gone?" Shuller itched for something to do. Susan was having none of it, however.

"No. It's been pretty quiet. Seems with you gone, everyone behaved themselves," she said.

"Probably they were just afraid of you, I suppose," he replied.

"I wish *you* were. Now, what was that about you going home and relaxing today?"

"How's the boy, Suz? I haven't seen David in ages." Shuller tried to derail the onslaught aimed at him. He figured bringing up her nine–year-old would slow down the verbal barrage.

"Good. Better, actually. I think he's finally coming to grips," she said softening up. David had a difficult time adjusting after his dad passed away from a sudden heart attack two years ago. "The season's opening game is tonight. He's really looking forward to it. You should be there. He's headed off to Mom and Dad's this weekend so it will be a chance for you to say hi. I'll bring him by the station sometime next week, you know, after you're *officially* back to work."

"Geez, just a regular dog with a bone." Shuller laughed. "Alright, alright. I'm gone. Guess those emails will have to wait till tomorrow."

"Exactly. Danny's been covering for you just fine." She smirked. "It really has been pretty quiet around here with you gone."

"I suppose that's good." *That only means something must be building in the wings somewhere*, he silently worried. "I best be off before you get the K-9s out." He slipped off the edge of her desk. "See you at the game," he said realizing he was not getting anywhere near his office. Shuller accepted defeat and began to make his way back toward the front desk. As he got closer, he caught Frank's eye.

"Told you you'd catch hell," Frank quipped under his breath.

"Didn't even make it past her desk," Shuller replied.

"I wouldn't think you'd have the chance there, boss! Did you?" he laughed. "So I'll catch you tomorrow then, boss?"

"Sure thing, Frank. Bye, Suzie Q," Shuller yelled over his shoulder as he pushed open the front door. He didn't turn to see her swat her hand at him as he left the station.

The hallway leading past his bedroom was still littered with boxes. *You never know how much crap you have until you move. And, you never remember where you packed anything*, he thought as he dug through a box deposited just outside the master bathroom.

"Where the hell is the extra toothpaste?" Levi muttered as he clawed at the box. After he had squeezed the last bit of life from the Crest tube, Levi was on the hunt for its replacement. "There you are, you son-of-a-bitch."

Box in hand, he returned to the bathroom. He tore into the box and made a half-assed attempt to brush his teeth. Levi had just started to settle into his routine after only moving to town a month ago.

Eventually, I'll finish unpacking.

He already started to blend well with the guys at the repair shop. Stepping into the shoes after Chuck retired as head mechanic was daunting to say the least. Forget about adding the fact he was new to town entirely. He worried the guys would resent him for leap frogging over one of them. Levi was thankful to be wrong. It was the fresh start he was looking for and so desperately wanted.

Levi finished up in the bathroom and headed down the hall to the kitchen. He swiped his keys and wallet off the counter and left through the side door. His baby waited for him in the driveway, a Mustang he was slowly refurbishing. She looked rough on the outside, but under the hood, she purred like a kitten. He locked the door and soon climbed in to his 'Stang and slammed the heavy door. He started her up and eased her back down the driveway.

He clicked on the radio. Billy Joel wafted through the speakers.

Hmm, they sound a bit tinny. I need to get those replaced next, he thought. Even still, he cranked up the volume and found himself drumming along to *Only the Good Die Young*. He roared up Crescent View Drive, pausing only for the light at Cedar Mill Lane. He hesitated before making the turn. While new to the town, he already knew one aspect that he was not very fond of already. His gut churned at the thought of passing the house, her house. *Just grin and bear it. We're doing fine*, he thought. He navigated around the corner, successfully avoiding looking at her house.

He made the light at Parker and cruised past the police station. He nodded at Shuller on the street as he approached the light at Emerson and the shop.

PRODIGAL SON

Try to get all neighborly with the locals, he thought. The Mustang bounded in the entrance ramp of the lot. Shocks were also on his list of repairs. The car roared as he drove around to the back of the shop and parked. Billy finished his song as Levi turned off the car. He climbed out, locked up, and dropped the keys into his blue jumper pocket. Levi strolled into the garage bay whistling while his keys faintly jingled in his pocket.

Shuller strolled down the street aimlessly. Susan was right about how he rarely had time off. She was usually right more often than not. Shuller was not one for taking extra time for himself. Not that he was needed at the station as often as he manned the desk. The town was never one to be riddled with crime. He just found it more comforting to be at the station. He felt it was more productive than hanging out at the house sitting in front of the television, unless it was football season.

The suggestion floating around his brain, Shuller realized he was indeed walking to Mitchell's Barber Shop. A ding of the door marked his entrance.

"Marty!" Mitchell greeted him instantly. "Good to see you."

"Hey, Mitchell. Figured I'd swing in to say hi. Susan already booted me from my office next door." He walked over to the aged barber for a quick hug and a pat on the back.

"You're not here for a cut, are you? I can practically see your scalp."

"Yeah, those personal clippers got the better of me," Shuller said, rubbing the top of his head again. His personal haircut seemed to highlight the appearance of the hint of grey he was starting to show.

"That's what you get. You leave that to me from now on, you hear?" Mitchell said, wagging his black comb at him. He returned his attention to his current customer draped in the smock.

"No problem. Apparently, I'm crap at it. How are you doing, Jim?" Shuller asked the gentleman perched in the chair. Shuller claimed the empty chair next to Mitchell's clipping station.

"Not too bad. Figured I'd have Mitchell tame the tumbleweed up there. Try to leave some, would you? I need what little I have left." They chuckled.

"You won't think it's so funny when it's your turn, son," Jim turned to Shuller.

"Why do you think I buzz it so close? I'm preparing for the inevitable. That way, it is not too much of a shock when I go full bald eagle."

"Been back long? Everyone here followed the stories in the paper about that Samantha girl," Mitchell said.

"Nah. Got in late yesterday and crashed. Stayed behind there a bit and helped them wrap up paperwork before I headed home." Shuller resigned to the fact that the story, while it was over from his perspective, would still be a source of discussion for some time. "Yeah. I figure I'll be talking about that for a bit before it finally goes away. I just figured I'd drop in and say hi to the guys now that I'm home, but Susan took care of that right quick. A much shorter visit than I had originally planned."

"Since Susan kicked you from your office, what do you have planned today, Marty?" Mitchell asked between snips of his long sliver scissors.

"I guess go home and start sorting through that pile of junk mail collected on my kitchen table. Suzie Q was nice enough to collect my mail, but she could have thrown out all that crap."

"Guess she figured to keep it for you so you'd keep out of her hair a bit longer," Mitchell replied.

"No pun intended, huh?" Shuller pointed at Mitchell as he rose from the chair. Mitchell smiled.

"Well, I'll leave you to it. I suppose I'll be seeing you in like 3-4 weeks then."

"Better make it more like 4-6," Mitchell said giving Shuller the once over. "You really did a number on that head," he chuckled.

"Uh, yeah." Shuller laughed. "See you around." Shuller waved at the two gentlemen as he left the shop. Shuller paused outside and took in the quiet.

Guess I'll just head home then, he thought. The wind carried with it the aroma of the corner bakery. The smell of fresh baked bread diverted his attention. The downfall of an active bakery on the corner from the place you spend a majority of your day, the constant smell of fresh baked goods played with your self-resolve.

"On second thought, I know where I'm headed next," he muttered. Shuller headed back up the street toward the bakery. He had a long lazy Sunday ahead of him, apparently. He didn't have the urge to rush home and do chores, despite the pile of laundry and yard work waiting for him. He slipped his hands in his pockets and meandered up the street once more. It just felt good to be home.

PRODIGAL SON

Chapter Two

The voices were barely audible, but he knew exactly what they were discussing on the other side of the heavy wooden door. He was to be placed in yet another foster home. This would be his fourth home in two years. He tried to make it work each time. He was not the one that was broken; it was the system. It was case after case where families sought state funds more than a child. There he sat, on a long empty bench in the hallway, awaiting his fate. *Would they be different? Will they even like me this time?*

He knew better by now than to get his hopes up. He knew how the world worked despite his young age. The nine-year-old sat silently, praying this time would be better. He eyed the varnish-cracked door. The footsteps approached the door besides him. He inhaled sharply. The door swung open, startling young Levi. He had barely steadied himself before the introductions started.

"Levi? I'd like you to meet Mr. and Mrs. Swanson. You'll be going home with them today," Ms. Donalds said. She had an almost painful painted on smile.

Levi knew that tone of her voice too well. He knew full well it was just an act. Ms. Donalds had sold him out again. Levi slipped off the bench, resigned to this new fate. He held out his little hand as he had been instructed to do many times before. The Swansons barely knew what to make of his zombie like motions.

"Hi." He looked up at them, blinking.

Mrs. Swanson had obstructed the view of the ceiling light of the hallway. It had framed her head in an eloquent glow. She had a kind face and greeted him with a warm smile. She gracefully took his hand.

"Well, hello there, Levi. Would you like to come home with us today?" Her voice was soft.

Levi stared at her. He had envisioned a harsher introduction to this next chapter of his life. Given his previous experiences, he had no reason to think this was his fairy tale ending. Mrs. Swanson, so far, was a pleasant surprise.

Mr. Swanson stood tall and strong beside her. He knelt down quickly, startling the boy. Levi retreated backward while removing his hand from Mrs. Swanson's grip. Mr. Swanson looked up at his wife with a look of concern.

"Hey, sorry there, son," he said trying to soothe the boy. "Didn't mean to frighten you there. Just wanted to get a better look at you is all." He too had a warmness about him.

Levi stood puzzled. *Were they actually different? Was this time going to be different from before?* Recovering again, he stepped forward and slowly offered his hand in introduction. Mr. Swanson gingerly accepted the greeting and returned the child an unassuming smile.

"Now, that's better," Mr. Swanson said sweetly. "Say, why don't you run off and get your belongings ready, huh? I'll take care of things here. Olivia," Mr. Swanson looked back at his wife, "why don't you and Levi head off to his room and help him get ready?" He released Levi's hand and rose from bended knee. She beamed back at him.

"Would that be okay?" she asked Levi. Wide-eyed and bewildered, he nodded. He slipped past the Swansons and Ms. Donalds and headed to 'his room' these past five weeks.

"Okay then. We're off. We'll see you in a few, George," she said and turned to follow Levi. Despite his initial sprint, Levi's pace slowed. Levi dredged down the semi-lit hallway with his chin planted on his chest. Levi half turned and caught a glimpse of Mrs. Swanson behind him. He noted the way the shadows rose and fell as they passed each overhead light fixture, the way her sweet perfume scented the air before her, washing over him.

Mrs. Swanson could not help but notice the peeling wallpaper. There were hints of spider webs in the upper corners of the doorways. They passed a few opened doors along their route. She took note of some kids scattered about, playing and drawing. She also took note of the lack of eye contact Levi made with them as they passed.

How does something like this still exist? she wondered. *This dinge and overwhelming solemnness is almost too much to bear. It's just heartbreaking to think of you here, sweet boy.* Mrs. Swanson felt ill at ease there.

She and her husband wanted to give a child the life they may not ever have had the chance of getting. The group home was a known, unfortunate, reality. The state run facility was barely possible as 'living'; however, it gave a roof over children's heads that would have otherwise been left to their own devices. Once the Swansons found out about the conditions of the home and listened to all the rumors of the corruption regarding its daily operations, they knew they had to foster and adopt from this place. They felt it was more like rescuing a child than merely fostering him.

Levi reached the door to his room and entered without ceremony. His room contained of four wooden framed bunk beds. Each bed was made with the pillows plumped and poised at the head. They were instructed to always present their rooms in a tidy and orderly manner at all times. At the foot of each bed sat two trunks. A paper tag hung from each of the oversized dented metal clasps. Levi headed directly to the first of the second set of trunks, his name scrawled across the tattered tag.

Mrs. Swanson had tentatively entered the room behind Levi. She did not interrupt him but cautiously circled past him and sat on the lower bunk and observed. The smell of disinfectant was almost palatable. She sat on the edge of the terribly soft mattress as she watched Levi lift the cumbersome lid to the trunk. There laid every earthly possession the nine-year-old had in this world. Inside the trunk were a few notepads, some comics, a stray stuffed toy or two, and a large plastic toy car, his prized possession. During his brief little life, he had learned to keep mementos to a minimum.

Levi rose up and crossed over to the closet where he kept his suitcase. He grabbed his checkerboard-patterned case and carried it over to the dresser. Mrs. Swanson just sat and watched. Sorrow crept over her as she soon came to realize the sad truth; he had done this many times before. She wanted to offer assistance but kept herself in reserve.

Levi loaded his clothes into his luggage rather quickly. His wardrobe, too, was on the conservative side. After he carefully laid his clothes in the case, he dragged it across the room to the trunk. He took each toy out one at a time and laid it across the neatly folded clothes. Mrs. Swanson sat in awe. She cocked her head to the side and caught the eye of the very determined nine-year-old. She offered a shy smile. Levi found himself returning the gesture before returning to the task.

A glimmer of hope, Mrs. Swanson thought.

Mr. Swanson appeared in the doorway. He motioned to his wife who quietly waved him off. She didn't want to disturb the process before her. He, too, silently observed as Levi continued to pack. He crossed his arms and leaned on the door jam. Levi was very methodical in his packing. Despite the brevity of the bounty, he took great care in its arrangement. Mr. Swanson stood and smiled at the boy. Levi completed his tasks and clicked the case closed. He sat and stared at the checkered pattern for a few moments.

How many times, already, he has seen that view, she thought. Levi raised his gaze from the case to Mrs. Swanson with a quick jerk of the head.

"All ready?" she asked.

Levi nodded.

"You want me to get that for you?" Mr. Swanson asked from the doorway.

Levi jumped, not realizing he was behind him. Mr. Swanson righted himself in the doorway, uncrossing his arms. He looked at his wife, at a loss for the boy's reaction again. She shook her head as she had little to offer as far as an explanation. Levi stood and turned to Mr. Swanson.

"Do you want me to?" he motioned to the luggage.

"O-Okay. Um, yes, sir," Levi stammered. It was the most he had said to the couple the whole time. Mr. Swanson gave him a wide smile, crossed over to Levi, and reached for the luggage handle. Levi, still a bit guarded, watched Mr. Swanson take the case. He heard the springs of the bed behind him creak. Soon, Mrs. Swanson stood beside her husband, both looking down at the child.

"Anyone you want to say goodbye to before we head out?" Mrs. Swanson offered. Levi smirked and shook his head no. His eyes dipped downwards. His friends, or what passed as friends, were long gone from the house. Mrs. Swanson looked up at her husband with a shrug.

"Well, guess that's it then," Mr. Swanson said. "After you," he said to Levi, sweeping his arm toward the door. Levi looked over at the door and then back at the Swansons. They stood there, both smiling. He tilted his head, regarding them for a mere moment. His mouth curled slowly into a meek smile. He turned and headed out of the room. Mr. and Mrs. Swanson followed.

"What was that all about?" Mr. Swanson whispered to his wife. They hung back slightly, discussing the poor emotional state of the child who edged closer to the front door.

"He damn near jumped out of his skin every time I spoke to him."

"The poor thing. Lord knows what has happened to him they haven't told us," she replied. "You remember the stories we heard about this place. I just hope it's not too late for him; that this place hasn't already broken his spirit."

"Did you notice the state of that room?" Mrs. Swanson continued. "Not exactly the Four Seasons, is it?"

"Did you expect it to be white glove ready, Liv?" he replied.

"Well, no. But really now. When the last time was that floor has seen a mop? The doorways had cobwebs, and the curtains were caked with dust along the top, for crying aloud. Ugh. If that is how they have him living here, I can only imagine where they placed him."

"Well, something happened to him somewhere along the line," he replied. "Of course they probably won't say anything, but it is apparent he's been abused or something. That Ms. Donalds doesn't strike me as the most trustworthy or forthcoming woman to be honest. She's more than happy to rent the kid out from what it seems. What I do know is he's been in the system since he was born. Not sure when they started placing him, or why he was not flat out adopted as a baby, but when you think about it, that's nine years of foster families and this place. That kind of life obviously has not been very good for him from the looks of it." He shuddered at the thought of it.

"Well, let's make this one the last family he's placed with then," she smiled up at him.

"Let's hope he lets us," he said back to her.

Levi stopped just short of the front doors. The faint tapping of raindrops could be heard against the concrete landing outside. Mr. Swanson pushed the front door ajar and peered around it.

"Looks like we can make it to the car before the heavy stuff hits," he said. "Wanna make a break for it?" he said nodding to Levi.

Levi smiled in spite of himself. Mr. Swanson jerked his head to the side and pushed his way through the door. Mrs. Swanson and Levi were quickly on his heels, trotting down the concrete steps to the street. Luckily, the car was only around the side of the building in the lot so it was not too much of a jog in the early storm mist.

Mr. Swanson had Levi's case tucked under his arm and rummaged for his keys in his front pocket. He made it to the car before his wife and Levi. He had the car unlocked just as Mrs. Swanson and Levi approached the door. He opened the backdoor,

Levi dove in and his case followed, while Mrs. Swanson made her way to the front passenger side and did the same. A slam or three of the car doors and all were inside and shaking off what little moisture they collected on their clothes.

"Everyone buckle up," Mr. Swanson said. He pulled himself around to face Levi in the backseat. "You got it?" he asked, checking on him.

"Yeah. Yes, sir," Levi replied as he clicked the belt secure.

"Alright then. Good. Let's go home then, huh?" He shot a quick smile to his wife and started the car.

Levi settled back into the plush seats of the car. As they backed away from the building, he watched as the building seemed to grow in the windscreen before them. Not even the rain could cleanse the dingy feeling Levi associated with that place. It was a feeling of loneliness and despair. He finally felt that, perhaps, he was leaving that all behind. The Swansons seemed to be a nice couple. Most foster parents drop the nice act by the time they hit the front door. *Maybe this time it was not an act.*

The lamps had just begun flickering to life as they merged onto the street. The droplets on the windows caught the light in a way they almost appeared like little diamonds. They illuminated and faded as they drove. As they approached the corner of the block, he watched how his diamonds turned into rubies, then soon into emeralds with the changing of the street light.

Mr. and Mrs. Swanson exchanged quiet glances. Every now and then, they would peer over their shoulder and check on their silent passenger. Levi simply watched the world go by outside the car window. He watched as the graffiti and boarded up abandoned buildings gave way to colorfully adorned storefronts with flower-boxed windows. The further they journeyed, the more Levi felt he was leaving behind the negatives of his past. Even the storm was behind him. He looked past his new foster parents out the front window to see blue skies ahead. The sentiment was not lost on the small child.

Though short, the drive from the facility to the Swansons home was certainly light-years from where he was just this morning. The storm had already passed through the area and the sun was making a reappearance. As Mr. Swanson pulled up the driveway and parked the car, Levi noticed how the sun gleamed off the wet surfaces, making everything look shiny and new. Mr. Swanson shut off the car and twisted sideways in his seat.

"Ready?" he asked.

Levi looked at Mr. Swanson before glancing out the window. He stared at a neatly trimmed green lawn and a quaint white house adorned with black shutters. He nodded eagerly, his eyes transfixed on the house. Both Mr. and Mrs. Swanson got out of the vehicle. Mrs. Swanson opened the backdoor just as her husband came around from the rear.

"Welcome home, Levi," she said softly. Tears welled in her eyes as she watched him ease from the car.

Levi stepped onto the walkway only half believing his eyes. None of his other foster family's houses looked like this one, ever. There was a small pathway leading to the front door. He gradually walked up the path to the door. It took the slam of the car door for the realization that he forgot his case behind him in the backseat. He turned to see both Mr. and Mrs. Swanson standing beside the car, Levi's case firmly in Mr. Swanson's hand.

They walked toward the house. Once again, Mr. Swanson jingled the keys and unlocked the front door. He swung it open wide and made way for Levi to enter. As Levi crossed the threshold, he caught the delicious smell of fresh baked cookies. He closed his eyes and inhaled deeply.

"I baked them before we left to pick you up," Mrs. Swanson said behind him.

Levi turned just as they walked in and closed the door.

"I thought it would be nice to come home to. You like chocolate chip?"

Levi again nodded eagerly. *Is this really happening?*

"So, you want the tour?" Mr. Swanson asked, placing Levi's suitcase down.

Levi was so lost in bewilderment that he didn't jumped when Mr. Swanson gently placed his hand on his shoulder to guide him through the house. He navigated the child through the downstairs layout. He walked him to the living room, dining room, and kitchen. Levi almost could not comprehend what he was seeing. This was fanciful to him. It was so outside the norm that he had experienced so far in his life.

"Wanna head upstairs?" he said, looking down at Levi.

"Yes," Levi responded quickly.

Mr. Swanson chuckled in response. "Well then, lead the way."

Levi found himself bounding up the stairs. His newfound enthusiasm was infectious as both Mr. and Mrs. Swanson quickly followed suit. Atop the stairs, Levi looked down a long hallway. It was a sharp contrast to the hallway at the facility. There it was dark and dreary. Here, the cream-colored walls were decorated with picture frames of smiling people, beautiful places, and happy events.

"Our room is here, but I'm pretty sure you'd like to see your room, huh?" Mr. Swanson said and received another eager nod from Levi. Mr. Swanson was glad to see the earlier jitters seemingly were left on the doorstep of the group home.

"Okay. Second door on the left." Mr. Swanson and his wife hung back as Levi ventured down the hall. They watched as Levi peered through the door as he came upon his room. He stood and took it in before turning his head to look back at them. Mrs. Swanson waved him to enter. Levi slipped into his new room.

It was clean and bright. Upon entering the room, he noticed the two large windows that opened to the back of the house, a twin bed staged between them. A tall dresser was to his right and a toy chest beside that. A door leading to his closet was on the far wall. There were random items perched on shelves and a small bookcase with several books resided next to his bed.

He was amazed. This room was bigger than the one he had just shared with three other boys. His head swept from one side to the other scanning and trying to understand what he was seeing.

"I hope you like it," Mrs. Swanson said from behind him. She swallowed and tried to hold back the tears in her eyes as she watched his head slowly bob up and down. Levi crossed over to the bed then turned to face the two of them.

"So I don't share this room with anyone else? It's all just for me?" It was the most he had said all at once all day.

"Yep, just you," Mr. Swanson said. "We hope you're going to be happy here, Levi. We've waited for you for a really long time." His voice was about to crack. He knelt down so his six-foot frame was at the boy's level. "I'll tell you something. We have to work through the system, but if you're happy and everything works the way I think it will, I think we'll all have a great life here."

Levi almost felt the urge to run and hug him, despite the feeling being foreign and unfamiliar to him. This whole situation was new. He had never been placed with a family that was well off as the Swansons. He was always the extra check that came in, the thing to have to deal with to be paid more. The families that had taken him in before were not the nicest or warmest of people. He typically found himself in virtually the same situation as he was in the group home. He often shared a room with two or three other kids. His clothes were hand-me-downs and the food was passible. That world was far removed from this. He was afraid he'd wake up and find himself back in that creaky, stain covered bed back at the facility.

"I bought you some new clothes," Mrs. Swanson said, breaking Levi from his fog. "They're in the closet there. I hope they fit."

New? Levi could not get to the closet any faster if he tried. He opened the door to find an assortment of clothes handing from hangers, their tags swinging from a breeze. Levi ran his hand across them, looking them over in astonishment. It was almost more than he could bear. He turned back to them watching him.

"Thank you," was all he could muster. The tears that had welled up in his eyes broke free and started to stream down his cheeks. That was all she needed before she, too, broke into tears.

"You're quite welcome, sweetheart," she stammered between sobs. Her husband squeezed her shoulders.

"Why me?" he asked.

"I'm not sure what you mean, dear," Mrs. Swanson said.

"Why did you pick me?"

Mr. and Mrs. Swanson stood lost for words momentarily. Finally, Mrs. Swanson broke the tension.

"Well, dear. We had been by a few times, actually. You hadn't noticed, but we came by for a few visits and observed the kids there, while you were outside playing. You seemed to need us," she said starting to choke up.

"You called out to us, without ever knowing you were doing it. We just knew you were the one."

Levi stood, trying to absorb the day. The Swansons were both in tears. Happy tears. A tender smile graced her face. Levi returned her smile.

"Why don't you take a few minutes to get accustomed to your room, Okay? Mrs. Swanson and I will give you a little privacy," Mr. Swanson said. He, too, felt that he would soon follow with his own tears.

Levi nodded, wiping the tears away with the back of his hand. Mr. and Mrs. Swanson slowly worked their way from the room, leaving Levi still scanning his new surroundings.

Levi checked out the remaining clothes that hung in the closet. He opened the chest of drawers where still more clothes were found all fresh and new. He walked over to the trunk and found new toys, all just for him. He stared out the large windows that overlooked the backyard. He stood at the window for a moment, his mouth agape. He inhaled sharply as he saw there was an in-ground pool. He had hit the kid version of the Lotto.

He moved toward his bed and pushed on the mattress. His hand sunk in the thick quilt on top. Levi noticed something rather quickly. There was no sound. The creaking of rusted metal springs was not there. Levi climbed up onto the bed. He kicked off his sneakers and swung his legs up. He sank back into the soft cushion of the pillow. His body melted into his plush surroundings. He had never experienced that before. Levi rolled onto his side, gathered the pillow in his arms, and hugged it tightly. Before he even realized it, he gave way to the exhilaration of the day and fell quickly to sleep.

Levi finally lived a charmed life, like one of the stories he had read. The rags to riches type of story that never really happens. In the coming weeks, the wall he cultivated over the years was slowly dismantled, one brick at a time.

His eleventh birthday was the best one ever. He had the party in the backyard complete with a large group of friends, but this year he got one gift he had always craved, a mom and dad. One week shy of two years, Levi and the Swansons were officially a family. The frail and meek child had a home and was never leaving.

After his adoption, Levi was a typical kid growing up. He had the usual kid difficulties. He was grateful to have the normal kid issues, though, grateful to have a normal life instead of having whatever living at the group home. Not only did he finally have parents, he had grandparents.

PRODIGAL SON

His grandparents lived outside of town on a modest farm. Many trips were made to their farm over the years growing up. While they were family, he was never as close to them as he would have been if he were blood, he felt. Still, it was more than he had ever had hoped to have in life.

While in high school, being an honor student was not exactly in the cards for him. He maintained the grades he needed to stay on the football team. His parents never missed a chance to see their favorite running back in action. After graduation, Levi found himself at a community college. He was content, and his parents were always supportive. It really was a great life. The first quarter of college already over, Levi was relaxing over the holidays at home with his folks. Life was good, but with all good things…

The Swansons were returning from a friend's home that New Year's Eve. They never arrived. An underage drinker too full of holiday spirits shattered Levi's world. Gone was the wholeness he found, the charmed life, his parents. Nineteen-year-old kidsshould not have to bury their parents. Levi was distraught, lost in his new reality. He began to withdraw. While there was a large support system for him, his serenity had died with his parents. The Swansons had been responsible enough to leave provisions in case of God knows what, so Levi had little to worry about financially, but what was a nineteen-year-old kid to do with a house, paid off or not. He struggled for some time for a foothold. College was no longer pressing for him. He battled back and created himself a decent living. He survived. Life moved on, and in time, so did he.

While he would move away, he could never bring himself to sell the family home. He kept the house and would return to it occasionally. He could not bear having anyone else live there either, so renting it out was never an option. He maintained the standards his parents set and ensured the house never fell into disrepair. He was still the dutiful son, despite his growing bitterness that stemmed from their passing.

Eventually, he would become a multiple homeowner after the passing of his grandparents. The grandparents' farm, however, did not rank very high on his priority list. As a kid, it was a great place to visit during the summer. The now mechanic had no business trying to be a ranch hand or managing any either.

He auctioned off the livestock and equipment, but never quite gotten around to selling the property out right. It was not much of a place, not very many acres for it to bring in a large return, honestly. Selling that house was on his list of things to do, however, it was at the bottom of a very long list. Over time, the house had become one of those abandoned home fronts driven past along a remote country road. Levi would one day come to visit his grandparent's home, but that day would be very, very long off.

Levi became the epitome of a blue-collar worker. He was of average height, weight, and everything else typical. He had rugged hands, callused and worn from hard labor. He felt he lacked the ability to manage his own life, forget about reminisces of other's lives. He was just the average guy living an average life. Nothing much remarkable about him to the naked eye.

PRODIGAL SON

Chapter Three

"Woo Hoo." Shuller cheered.

David had caught a fly ball and Shuller rose to his feet. The baseball game was tied. With runners in scoring position, getting the out was crucial. The defending Little League champions were in fine form. The buoyant boys of summer were starting to hit their stride again going into the bottom of the fifth inning.

"Heck of a game," Shuller said exuberantly.

Susan smiled. The field's stands were packed with cheering parents and fans. Ever the sports enthusiast, Shuller never missed the Huntersville Heat play. Susan laughed at his vocal support more than cheering for her own child.

"You're going to hurt yourself if you're not careful," she jested. "Now sit your fool ass down."

"Just showing the team some love, Suz." He smiled back at her. "They're getting their groove back. Gonna be another great year!"

"Listen to you. It's the first game of the season. Surprised you're not president of the boosters."

"You know, I thought about it. Couldn't get around the fact that not having a horse of my own in the race, seemed a little odd," he quipped.

"A horse, huh? Fine euphemism for a kid, Martin."

"You know what I mean. Heck, in this day and age, a single grown man volunteering to play with a bunch of kids he has no real connection to, well, that may come off as peculiar."

"Yeah, you perv," Susan chuckled and shook her head. Just then, the warm evening breeze brought with it the scent of freshly popped popcorn.

"Hey, flag him down." She nudged Shuller. "Get us some, would you?"

Shuller followed her gaze and saw the red shirt of the wandering vendor. "What do you think this is, a date?" He laughed. "I'll flag him down, but that's about it."

"Some gentleman you are. And to return the offense, good God no; this is not a date."

"I wasn't that offensive," he replied. "I guess I could spare the cost of a bag."

"I would think. Being the best secretary you've ever had, I should be good enough to score a bag of popcorn" she ribbed him again.

"You're the only secretary I've ever had." Shuller smiled and raised his arm. The vender spotted him right off and made his way over. Two dollars and fifty cents later, Susan started munching away at her popcorn.

"So, we friends again?" he asked sarcastically.

"Sure, I suppose," Susan mumbled with a mouth full of popcorn. "So," she swallowed and continued, "since you brought up dating, I have a question."

Shuller shot her a quick look.

"Oh, don't give me that look. Not with me, you ninny. We already covered that. Have you given any more thought about Jeanie?"

Jeanie Jacobs worked as the fire station's dispatcher. Right before Shuller went out of town for what turned out to be weeks longer than he ever had planned, Susan started laying down the groundwork for a possible connection between the two. Susan and Jeanie struck up a friendship a long time ago. They found a kinship as they both worked the public service sector. While Shuller was gone, she worked on Jeanie and got her on board with her plan. Getting Jeanie to agree was not much of a challenge as it turned out. Shuller was, as Susan had often described to Jeanie, "a catch." Susan promoted Shuller as the single six foot-one town sheriff who had a "nice build and was easy on the eyes." Jeanie didn't require much priming. With Jeanie's buy in, Susan's efforts turned to working on Shuller.

"You two would get along great. She's funny and smart, and single."

"Oh, okay, good. Afraid I would have to deal with a jealous husband or boyfriend," Shuller said dismissively. "So, we're back to this again, huh?"

"Oh, come on, Jeanie is great and you know it. And she's an avid football fan," Susan sing-songed to him. "I believe a Pats fan and everything," Susan said, trying to appeal to his favor with the mere mention of his favorite team.

"Hmmm. A Pats fan, really?"

Susan smiled wide.

"Now is she a fan, or does she like football? There is a big difference." Shuller's interest was piqued a bit.

"Oh, a fan. She loves sports, in fact." Susan looked off down the steps of the bleachers. "She is also a fan of a particular little league team, in fact." Susan caught the eye of the inbound set up.

Shuller noticed Susan's distant gaze and focused his eyes in the same direction. He quickly realized what was happening, albeit too late to avoid it.

"Suz," he whispered urgently under his breath.

Susan merely returned his stern look with a grin. "What? She was coming to the game anyway after her shift. I told her to find us. Not a biggie, right?" She was grinning ear to ear.

Shuller inhaled sharply and tried to cover his growing dismay. He was glad the stands were packed. That meant it took her a bit longer to get to him and gave him more time to prepare for awkward pauses and broken conversations. Despite the crowd, Jeanie found her way to their riser rather quickly.

"It's about time you got out there," Susan said through a tightly stretched smile.

Shuller had the innate feeling to run. The crowded bleachers had become a disadvantage. Shuller gave Jeanie a tight smile of his own while he relished the thought of when he could pay Susan back for this kindness.

He suddenly felt cumbersome and out of his depth. He was the town's sheriff, a leader. The mere thought of talking to a woman made him vulnerable. It was not a feeling he liked or was used to.

This is ridiculous, he thought. *She's going to sit here; we'll exchange pleasantries and call it a day. Lord knows what Suzie Q built this up to be.*

Susan jumped up and gave Jeanie a quick hug. She graciously offered Jeanie the seat next to Shuller.

Nice one, Suz. Shuller rose slowly.

"Thanks, hun," Jeanie said to Susan as she scooted by her. "Hi, Sheriff."

"Martin," he replied. Martin. It sounded so foreign to him. He was more accustomed to Sheriff or Shuller. He scooted aside as she took her seat on the bench beside him. She returned the favor with a brief shy smile. Shuller felt clunky and disjointed. Jeanie was very disarming. Again, not something he was accustomed to either. The evening breeze carried the soft floral scent of her perfume. Shuller inhaled the intoxicating scent before he awkwardly attempted a conversation.

"All quiet at the station?" *Good one, Marty. Talk shop!*

"I could ask the same of you," she replied with a smile. "Thankfully, yes. It hasn't been that dry of a season, so there have been no big issues. It's been just the typical rescuing kittens stuck in trees kinda week."

Shuller chuckled.

Just then, the Heat's batter smashed a curve ball. The crowd roared to life as the pintsized runner rounded first.

"He got a hold of that one, didn't he?" Jeanie said emphatically. "Oh, look, Davey is up next. I got here just in time. Between him and the kid they got on deck, we're looking at pulling ahead here."

"You really are into sports, huh?" Shuller said. A couple of baseball buzzwords and Shuller became intrigued.

Susan tried not to appear too interested, but did steal a few glances at the two. She stifled a smile knowing that sports would be Shuller's undoing. She found it difficult as her attentions were diverted between watching her son stride to home plate and eavesdropping on her project in progress besides her.

"Oh, yeah. I'm more of a football fan, but when it comes to Davey, I'll make room for some baseball."

"I know what you mean. Speaking of Davey," Shuller said motioning to the field.

Davey, huh? Susan thought. Shuller was more formal usually. *What happened to David? Gee, that was fast.* Susan could not hide her smile since her plan to get the two to bond over baseball seemed to be working.

The three sat and watched intensely as David approached the plate. Poised and ready, David's bat hovered over his shoulder, just like all the players he watched on TV. The first pitch came high and fast; strike one.

"Seriously?" Shuller exclaimed. "That was damn near his head."

"Easy there, boss," Susan said, reaching to pat his arm. "But, yeah, what the hell?"

PRODIGAL SON

The second opportunity would not be a repeat of the first as David's bat cracked loud upon contact. The three bounded from their seats as David dropped the bat and took off for first. His little legs carried him right round the bag, and he aimed for second. Out of the corner of his eye, he caught sight of the ball thrown from the outfield. Within a few feet of the bag, he hit the dirt and slid. The umpire called safe before the dust had a chance to settle. The crowd vociferously agreed with the call. The home team now had a man on second and third.

"There you go," Jeanie exclaimed. The three clapped wildly and hollered along with the rest of the crowd.

"If Joshua can repeat that, we'll start pulling ahead now that Michael's on third," Susan added

"Heck, even if he draws a walk, it will be bases loaded. They only have the one out so far; if they keep getting base hits then they'll start racking up the runs in no time flat," Shuller said.

Susan, who was a bit horse from cheering, spied on the two huddled together, discussing the next several pitches. *This plan just works itself,* she thought proudly. *Barely had to do a thing other than slide over!*

The next four innings flew by. Shuller and Jeanie spent the time playing manager. The three of them cheered as the Heat claimed victory. The stands cleared. Susan started filing out with the crowd, followed by the chatty twosome. They walked down the concrete steps of the bleachers toward the field. David, fresh from the celebratory mosh pit on the pitcher's mound, found his mom headed down the aisle.

"Hey, Mom!" he yelled.

Susan smiled proudly and waved. She pointed toward the dugout and continued her way down the steps. Shuller and Jeanie were oblivious to this exchange as they continued recounting the plays of the game in their version of Sports Center. They blindly followed Susan's lead and soon made their way to the chain link fence separating the stands from the field. David had run over to the fence by the dugout and met them as they approached.

"Great game, bud!" Susan exclaimed as they came face to face.

"Fantastic play in the bottom of the fifth there, little man," Shuller chimed in. "What I'd tell you? Open up that mitt more and that stance and look what happens."

"So that was a result of your coaching, huh?" Jeanie egged Shuller.

"I'd like to think I had a hand in it. Oh, and I'm sure his coach may have had something to do with it," he conceded, if only slightly.

"Well, head on in," Susan urged David. "We'll meet you around back."

David bounded into the dugout. Susan, Shuller, and Jeanie plodded out with the crowd as it spilled into the parking lot. The three collected at the back entrance to the team's dugout and waited for the second baseman. They didn't have to wait long. David's energy propelled him out the doorway and toward them. He broke into a full on run headed toward his mom.

"Whoa," Susan said as the two connected. "Almost knocked me over there, hun. How do you still have energy?"

"We killed it tonight!" David was still flying high from the recent win.

"Yeah, we saw," Jeanie chimed in. "That was some awesome catch there! Really impressive, Davey. Up for some pie at the diner?"

"Yeah!"

"Um, no. Not tonight, I'm afraid. It's late enough as it is, bud," Susan interrupted. "And your grandfather is coming over to pick you up tomorrow. I don't feel like dragging you out of bed in the morning."

"Geez, Mom, what a buzzkill," Shuller jested. Jeanie stifled a laugh. Susan noted how out of character it was for him. She smiled, thinking it was more for Jeanie's benefit than it was to razz her.

"If you ever had to damn near set off an M80 to get him up in the morning, then you would feel my pain."

"Sorry, guy, but Mom overrules," Jeanie said. "It will have to be another time though, for sure."

David shrugged. He knew there was no argument that would overturn the verdict.

"We'll have a celebratory pie when you get back from your grandparents then," Shuller said.

"Sure thing, Sheriff," David said.

"Speaking of heading out," Susan said, prodding David toward the car. She smiled down at the boy who was now beaming at the thought of pie.

"We won't keep you. You need to get to bed, young man. A well-earned rest," Shuller offered.

Susan nodded and then grinned at them. There was more behind the smile than gratitude for supporting her son. There was the knowledge that her mission had been a roaring success. She guided her son toward the car, leaving Shuller and Jeanie standing together in the parking lot.

My work here is done, she thought as she and David reached her car.

"Davey can't get some pie, but there's nothing saying we can't," Jeanie ventured, seeing if Shuller would bite at the invitation.

"Mmm, pie," Shuller muttered. "I could go for some pie about now." Shuller felt uneasy again. It was the awkward pre-teen jitters he got before asking a girl to dance. Shuller suddenly didn't know where to look, how to hold himself. He was acutely aware of the weight of his own body. He gave Jeanie a shy smile, something that rarely made an appearance.

"What do you say we head over?" Jeanie continued to coax an answer from the shy sheriff.

"Couldn't see why not." *Well that was classy Martin. Make a girl feel special, why don't you.* "Uh, you drive or walk over from the station?"

"Walk. My car's over in the lot. You?"

"Same. It's a nice night for a stroll over to the diner."

"Sounds great." Jeanie smiled.

PRODIGAL SON

The cloudless summer's evening was the perfect backdrop for a slow stroll to the diner. A small faction of the crowd lingered about while others meandered to their cars. A few also decided a trip to the diner was in order. Several people wandered up the street ahead of them as they embarked up Emerson Street. With the dissection of the night's game behind them, the art of casual conversation seemed to elude Shuller.

As they leisurely walked along the street, their arms would occasionally brush against each other. The casual chance contact would send chills up Jeanie's arm to the base of her neck. Shuller would practically freeze in what could be confused for sheer panic rather than the general thrill of a first date, which this evening had turned into it seemed.

Shuller did his best to keep the conversation going. He sputtered on randomly about current events, trying to avoid work. He didn't think he'd impress her with cop shop. The problem was he already ran the gamut of sports, what little politics he knew of, as well as the weather. It killed about ten minutes.

"So, are you an action adventure kinda movie goer or a drama guy?" Jeanie figured she would save Shuller from trying to carry the conversation.

"Hmm. I have enough drama at work most days." He chuckled. "I do enjoy a good explosion every now and again."

"Typical guy." Jeanie laughed.

"Well, yeah. I do like a variety of movies though," Shuller continued.

"Let me guess. Drama's out, so I'll say you typically go for action, mystery, suspense kind of movies."

"Yeah. Occupational hazard creeps in there a bit when it comes to my entertainment choices. I do enjoy a good comedy and some sci-fi."

"What, no westerns?" Jeanie jested.

"Nah. No westerns or martial arts either. Not much of a fan. I do like horror, but the best time of year to watch those is around Halloween."

"Oh, I know. Something about the cooler weather and a creepy movie," Jeanie said.

"There's nothing like freaking yourself out for no good reason." They shared a laugh.

"Alright. So no westerns or martial arts flicks. What about the tough-guy killer, then? Chick flicks. What's your opinion of rom coms?"

"Guys can like those," he replied. "Just not by themselves. Those are kind of a date thing in my book. That way you can say you were dragged to it despite wanting to see it," Shuller said.

Jeanie gave him a swat on the arm and a smirk. "So I'll have to *drag* you to see one then, is what you're saying?"

"That's what I'll tell people anyway." He snickered. *That sounds promising*, he thought.

"Here we go," Shuller said suddenly, trying to distract himself from the realization, she had started laying down the foundation for future dates. They had reached the diner before he realized it. He stepped forward and grabbed the door handle.

"After you," he said sweeping his arm across him.

Jeanie smiled and entered the diner. The smell of warm apple cobbler greeted them as Shuller quickly followed her inside. Jeanie led the way to a booth along the windows. Shuller slipped in across from her.

"Oh, that smells great," Jeanie said. "They have the best pies, I swear."

"Apple or cherry?" Shuller asked, continuing their preferences conversation.

"Hmm, apple. But only when it's warm."

"Good call."

"Hello, Sheriff, Ms. Jeanie," Terry said with a smirk. Jeanie gave her a quick *knock it off* twitch of the head. Terry acknowledged and dropped the tease before Shuller caught on.

"What can I get you to start? Coffee? Tea?"

"I'll have hot tea, Terry. Martin?"

"Coffee, please. Thanks, Terry." *I'm sure to hear about this at the office tomorrow,* he thought. Not only would Susan grill him mercilessly, Frank would surely join in once his wife tells him whom she waited on after the game. He started to realize he would not mind it so much.

"So a tea drinker?" Shuller said.

"Yes. Coffee in the morning, tea in the evening. Never knew why, but that always made sense to me," Jeanie offered.

"I can understand that. I'm a coffee guy. That is unless I'm at Viv's. Then it's English Breakfast or Earl Grey."

"Oh yeah. Susan told me how you visit with her. That's nice of you."

"Well, she's on her own now, and I worry that's becoming more and more of a bad idea. She's getting on in years and not as nimble as she used to be," Shuller said, hardly masking the concern in his voice.

"So she doesn't have any family around or does she not have any at all?"

"Not to be flippant, but she doesn't have any family that I know of left," he replied. "Of all our conversations, she's never recounted any relatives who are still with us."

"Such a shame. Her being in that house by herself like that," Jeanie said.

"Yeah, I know. That's why I make it a point to check in on her. Kinda in the same boat myself. Don't really have any family around here. Fortunately for me, though, I still have family. Even more fortunate, they live back on the East coast." He chuckled.

"Oh, you're awful!" Jeanie admonished. "Okay, spill. Where and who."

"Well I have a brother in New York. Manhattan really. He's married with two kids. And I have a sister, also married with three kids. She lives in upstate New York."

"Younger or older?"

"Aren't we inquisitive tonight?"

"Well, how else am I going to get info out of you?" Jeanie laughed.

"Brother older, sister younger."

"So, you're the middle child."

"Yep, I'm a sufferer of middle kid syndrome. It doesn't help that both are married with kids. I get crap for that all the time."

"I bet. I have an older sister. She's married with her first kid. I swear, as soon as she found out she was pregnant, she started in on me."

"What's that about?"

"Right?" Jeanie said. "It doesn't work like that. I wasn't even dating anyone at the time either."

They laughed as Terry reappeared with their cups.

"Here's your tea. Cream and sugar's on the table." Terry motioned to the far edge of the table as she placed the coffee cup in front of Shuller.

"Thanks, Terry." Shuller paused momentarily from their laughter. "What's the pie de jour? Smells like apple."

"A fresh apple cobbler just out of the oven," Terry replied as if she herself made it.

"What do you say? Warm apple cobbler," Shuller teased Jeanie.

"Mmm, definitely," she responded, nodding at Terry.

"Make that two," Shuller tagged on.

"Two cobblers, I'll be right back," Terry said, scribbling as she walked away.

"I'm not asking too many questions here. Kind of unfair," Shuller said, trying to get a reprieve from the investigation.

"I've given as much as I got, I think. Besides, you know whatever you don't get from me, Susan will gladly fill you in. Probably whether you want it or not." Jeanie laughed.

"You have a point."

"Besides, everyone else seems like an open book compared to you," she said taking a sip of her tea.

"And that's a bad thing?" Shuller asked.

"It is when you're on a date. You do realize that's what the whole meet up was about right?" Jeanie snickered.

"Oh yeah. The minute she said you were coming to the game, I knew," Shuller said. Despite her inquisitive nature, he didn't mind being set up so much.

"Surprised you didn't bolt from the stands," Jeanie said, gauging his reaction.

Shuller nervously laughed given that had crossed his mind at the time.

"Guess I could take that as a good sign of you wanting to meet me." Jeanie smiled. She knew the statement would throw him a bit. She liked that he was off balance. It was refreshing to see the steel-nerved sheriff thrown for a loop.

"So, you have more questions I assume?" Shuller asked, diverting the implication he secretly wanted to meet her. An admission like that was too close to home.

"So," Jeanie continued, "let's see what I've got so far. You're a Pats fan, a middle child, an uncle, and coffee drinker. You like warm apple cobbler and you're a transplanted New Yorker. Hmm, not bad for a few minutes, but you're going to have to cough up more."

"More?" Shuller rebuked. "It takes weeks for most people to get half that out of me." Shuller chucked in spike of himself. "Transplanted New Yorker?"

"Well your accent has faded a bit, but the fact your siblings 'live back on the East coast' kind of gives it away." She smirked. "Besides, not many people outside New York say 'upstate'."

"You got me there. Yeah, I moved away a long time ago."

"How long was 'long time ago'?"

"Didn't realize I stepped into an integration room," Shuller said, pushing back from the table.

"No one expects the Spanish Inquisition," Jeanie replied.

"Oh, a Monty Python reference. Nice," Shuller commended.

"You haven't answered my question yet."

"Ah, yes. When did I vacate New York? Let's say, God was a child when I left the Empire State."

"Hmm, I smell a story."

"Do you work part-time for the paper or something?"

"Nope. However, I am working on a book, and you're holding up Chapter 2. So, what gives?" She gave him a sly smile.

"Huh. That's a story for another time, maybe."

"That is soooo not a deterrent, but I'll let you slide on that." Jeanie sensed that she may have come too close to a nerve and decided to drop that line of questioning. "For now."

The smell of approaching cobbler put the questions on hold. Terry placed two large helpings before each of them.

"Enjoy," Terry said, once again, shooting Jeanie a guilty smile.

"Oh, we will, Terry, thanks," she replied, also returning a shy grin. Terry turned and left them alone in the booth by the window as they both swooned over more than just pie.

PRODIGAL SON

Chapter Four

The chair creaked *welcome home* to Shuller as he settled behind his desk.

It seems like forever since I've been back, he thought.

Shuller looked around the room. Everything was how he left it. Good thing, too. He didn't need his OCD to kick in and become preoccupied with putting things back in their place before he was ever able to get back to work. Despite the pending stack of paperwork to read, there was not much left to do for the day. It, indeed, was that quiet of a town.

There was a neatly stacked pile of manila folders in his outbox on the corner of the desk. Susan knew better than to file them before he had a chance to review and catch up. They were each very thin folders. Nothing catastrophic seemed to have happened while he was gone. Not that something major happened often around there, but Shuller got the feeling they were overdue. He could not help but sense it was in the air. After coming off the Harrigan case, it was hard not to expect to be blindsided again.

"Everything's just where you left it boss," Susan said, leaning in the doorway. "I knew better to mess with anything, or I'd hear about it for weeks like the last time."

"I wouldn't go on for weeks," Shuller shot back, startled a bit by her entrance. She was a welcomed interruption from his hopefully unfounded concern of the unexpected. "And what do you mean like last time? When did I ever just go off about filing paperwork?"

"Oh my God, you complained for just about a week after I filed when you were out sick. You drove me nuts saying how you like to review everything before I put them away, big or small, it didn't matter. You harped on it forever."

"When I was out...Suz, seriously? That was like three years ago," Shuller replied. "Are you trying to tell me you remember me 'going off' about some paperwork three years ago?"

"That's exactly what I'm saying. It was that memorable of an experience," she quipped. "This time, I left all the files on your desk, in order in which they occurred, so you review the events as they unfolded. Didn't want to listen to that again." She grinned.

"Well, it's much appreciated, Suzie Q," Shuller acknowledged. "And I wasn't that bad."

"Psh, oh please," she said. Susan stood quiet for a moment, her arms folded, fingers wrapping on her arm. The suspense was eating her alive. The fact that she held out as long as she did even surprised her. She could not hold back any more. The floodgates opened, and Susan wasted no time to start in on Shuller. "Sooo...." she continued to Shuller's dismay, "how'd things go after David and I left last night? You and Jeanie hit it off?"

Shuller inhaled sharply. The oncoming line of questioning he suspected was almost as uncomfortable as the set up itself. There was not much to tell, well nothing that would satisfy her inquisitive nature, he figured. She was going to want a play-by-play. Again, it was not his style to kiss and tell. Hell, there was no kiss to tell about, really.

"It was fine. We walked to the diner and had some pie."

"That's it? A walk and some pie? Are you kidding me?" Susan questioned. The disappointment was evident on her face.

"Well, yeah. What else did you expect? You kind of sprung that on me. There was not any time to prepare for a whirlwind romantic evening. I didn't have time to spin through the rolodex to line up a date night to beat all date nights, especially since I didn't know I was going to be on a date."

"The fact that you used the word rolodex in that sentence proves it has been way too long since you were on a date. It wasn't that late when we left. You could have taken her out somewhere."

"I did. We went to the diner." Shuller smirked. "The diner counts as somewhere, Suz."

Susan did have a point about it being a long time since he was on a date. He hadn't really made the time to date. He left that part of his life behind when he moved several years back.

Shuller shifted in his seat and grimaced knowing this conversation would not end until she got some tidbit out of him.

"Pie?" Susan stood, arms opened, waiting for those precious little details Shuller was far too uncomfortable to give. That didn't stop her from trying to pull the information from him. "There had to be more than just pie! Spill or I call Jeanie right now, on speaker, at my desk."

"Alright, alright. We walked to the diner and she quizzed me all the way. We basically took turns playing twenty questions." He sighed. "She got more questions in than I did, actually." A faint smile crossed his face.

Susan noticed it instantly. "Oh, I see. So, you were nice, right?"

"What do you mean by that?" Shuller asked, puzzled again. "Of course I was nice. Just because you bombarded me with a surprise, date doesn't mean I would be anything other than nice to the woman. Was I nice?" Shuller scoffed.

"You answered her questions, right? You tend to be a tightly sealed book, you know. You didn't grill her, did you?"

"Whoa, slow down there, Suz." Shuller threw up his hands. "I answered her questions, even volunteered some information. And, no. I did not grill her. It's funny how you don't seem to mind me saying how she grilled me though. Hmmm."

"Well it's part of your job to grill people. I just want to make sure you weren't too carried away or anything. Occupational hazard and all. She is a lovely lady. I wouldn't *bombard* you with someone who wasn't, you know," Susan replied, easing off a bit.

"She's quite the lovely lady, and we had a lovely time. We talked, had some pie, and I walked her back to the firehouse to her car."

"Okay then." Susan raised her eyebrows as she tilted her head.

"Is there something else on your mind, Suzie Q?"

"I was wondering if there was a second date discussed. With all that talking, you *did* talk about a next time, right?"

Shuller smiled in spite of himself. He again adjusted in his chair.

"We did discuss going out again. While I was walking her back to the car, I suggested perhaps we go out on a real date."

"That was a real date," Susan said, straightening her stance, offended by the remark. "Well, I mean, you could have treated it as if it was a real date." She realized quickly she tipped her hand more than she planned.

"Well, one of *our* choosing. One where we're both aware there's a date, if you will." He shot her a look out of the corner of his eye.

"Good then. Glad this all worked out. See? I told you you'd like her." Susan beamed.

"Yes. Good thing, too, since she only works down the block, and I'll see her practically every day. No pressure or anything, right Suz?" Shuller shot back.

"I'm good. Damn, I'm good." Susan could not hide her pride.

"Oh, will you get the hell out of here so I can do some work?"

"Whatever you say, boss. Do you need me to dust off that rolodex for you before you see Jeanie again? I wouldn't want you to choke on a decade's worth of dust or anything."

Shuller gave her a deadpan look. Susan shrugged her shoulders and left his office. He heard the faint giggle of a very pleased secretary returning to her desk.

Shaking his head, Shuller took a deep breath. He reached for the top folder in his outbox, slipping it off the stack. He leaned back in his chair and flipped open the folder. It was just a minor traffic infraction. There was nothing of significant interest in the file. More of the same followed. There was a fender bender, a few more traffic citations, and general benign-ness. There were no major anything that happened in the time he was gone.

Danny had a cakewalk while I was gone, he thought. *Good.*

Not that Shuller wanted anything bad to occur outside his watch, but if something did, he wanted to be the one to handle it. Ever the control freak, Shuller felt responsible for many things in town. He would not want the burden of something bad happening and not being there to help handle it.

Shuller closed the last of the folders and threw it onto the stack in the middle of his desk. Quick reads all of them. Shuller pressed his hands to his face and inhaled. He then ran his hands over his forehead and then down over his cheeks. He sat in the quite of his office. There were just random murmurs outside his office door. It was the typical office sounds of his station that he had missed. The unintelligible conversations and disembodied laughter from the guys soothed him. He turned and gazed out the window at the park across the street. A brightly colored kite tail caught his eye as it whipped in the breeze.

His thoughts wandered back to the night before, post pie. The walk to the fire station was only a five-minute walk, but it felt like an hour. A very well spent hour. The conversation flowed a bit more fluidly than it had all night, something Shuller was afraid would not happen without the aid of a few beers. Somewhere along the way, he dropped his guard. He relaxed, more so than the first instance of seeing her at the ball game. Jeanie had resumed her questioning as they walked. Shuller didn't mind so much now. He began to realize how he liked hearing her voice.

PRODIGAL SON

"You know, I should bring you in as a consultant on some of the really tough cases we get at the station," he broke into her latest effort for information. "I think you'll get a perp to crack within two minutes with this technique of yours," Shuller laughed.

"Hmmm. The *really tough* cases, huh? Like when Billy holds strong and refuses to flip on his buddy on the great candy caper?" Jeanie asked referencing when two junior high kids were caught shoplifting at the local grocery store.

"Well, yeah! That took incredible amounts of man-hours to put to bed! You have no idea. It made the papers didn't it?" Shuller teased. The two laughed. "Sad that is considered a big crime around here. Or rather I guess that is a good thing in the end."

"True. That's a big change from back East, huh?"

"To say the least, yes. I guess that's what drove me out this way. There was just too much everything there for me after a while. I miss it, sure, but at the end of the day, I needed nice and quaint. You know?"

"Nice and quaint? Hmmm. Not many guys say that, but yeah, I get what you mean. I'm a transplant, too, but not as far as New York. I was the opposite end of the country from your hometown; San Francisco, California."

"Oh really? I didn't see that coming."

"Yep. San Fran was nice, but apparently not what I was looking for either."

"Funny when you think about it, us being from either end of the country meeting out here in the middle of nowhere."

"Very true. What luck, huh?" Jeanie said, smiling at Shuller. "I do love it here, though. Nothing bad seems to happen here, really."

"Well, now you've done it!" Shuller replied.

"What do you mean?"

"Tempting fate like that. It's dangerous stuff putting something like that out into the universe. *Nothing bad happens here.* I might have to start doing some hard hitting police work now that you threw that out there."

"Oh, will you quit? You don't believe in stuff like that do you?"

"I can seem very matter of fact about most things, but when it comes to something like that, I'm a firm believer. Murphy's Law, karma, stuff like that, yeah, that comes around eventually I think."

"Now I didn't see that coming. You surprised me, Marty," Jeanie said.

"Look at that, I got one," he laughed.

"Well if something does break loose, I'll lend a hand, you know, to help cut down on the resource drain for you and the boys," Jeanie smiled at Shuller. He returned the smile. She took the opportunity to loop her arm around his. He accepted the gesture and clasped her hand with his. This was practically first base for him, or that's what it felt like. He continued to smile as he looked toward the ground. He raised he gaze back at her and caught her looking back.

PRODIGAL SON

They had been walking in auto pilot mode and before they realized it, they were on the corner of Parker, across from the firehouse. The parking lot lay before them. They turned the corner and continued down the nearly vacant street toward the lot. There were random people about on the street, filing into cars. The lights from the baseball field glowed in the distance, piercing the dark like a beacon. They arrived at the parking lot and Jeanie lead the way to her truck.

"Nice." Shuller gave his approval as they came up on the driver's door. He gave the older model pickup a once over. The dark blue truck had seen better days, but she still looked good.

"Yeah, she's got some miles on her, but I love my old girl." There was a few seconds of silence.

Shuller swallowed hard and figured he'd break the quiet. "This was an unexpected, but very pleasant, evening. Perhaps we can plan a night out, one where Suzie Q doesn't leave me out of the details?" *Man, I am rusty at this.*

Jeanie chuckled. "I would love that, Marty." Suddenly, she felt sixteen again. She fiddled with her key ring and unlocked her car door.

No key fob. She is an old girl, he noticed about the truck.

"I had a great time tonight. Thanks for being a sport, you know, with Susan and all."

"I've known Suzie for years. It comes with the territory." Shuller leaned over and opened her door for her. The heavy metal door creaked. Jeanie responded to his gallant gesture with a hug and a quick peck on the cheek.

"Look forward to next time," she said, her voice full of promise.

"Me, too. And I think I can speak on behalf of Suzie as well. Drive safe." Shuller watched her climb into the cab and closed the door behind her. He took a few steps back as she started up the truck. He waited for her to pull out from the parking spot and turn onto Parker before he started to his car at the station.

Shuller sat in his car, lost in thought, remembering the smell of her perfume from just moments ago; how the streetlamps caught the edges of her hair, framing her in this translucent glow.

Perhaps I shouldn't have dismissed Suzie so quickly before, he thought.

This was, apparently, a long time coming, at least from Susan's perspective. Here he was daydreaming of her back in his office. He recounted the evening in his head.

Should I have tried to kiss her goodnight? Nah. It wasn't a full on date. Was it?

The knock on the door jarred him out of his daydream.

"Sorry, I couldn't get to that dusting quick enough, boss, but you have a visitor." A voice came from the doorway. He turned to see Susan escorting Jeanie into his office. Shuller bolted to an upright position as if he was an errant child caught with his hand in the cookie jar.

"What? Oh, uh, thanks Suz," he said flustered.

"You need me to get you anything before I leave?" Susan asked with a smirk. She seemed to love to watch the sheriff squirm. She loitered in the doorway, rocking back and forth ever so slightly.

"Ah, no. We're fine, Suz. Thanks," Shuller said, coming around his desk to usher her out of the room.

Susan gave him a look as he approached. Shuller threw her a quick jerk of the head, and Susan stifled a giggle. She gave a small wave to Jeanie and left without much more persuasion.

"Hope I'm not interrupting," Jeanie said.

"Uh, no. No. Not at all. I'm just catching up on my reading from when I was gone," Shuller said as he pointed to the stack of files on his desk.

"Oh, seems like a lot of paperwork. I should probably let you get back to it."

"I've already reviewed them, really," he added, ensuring she would not leave. "They're all closed and old news anyway. I was just playing catch up is all. So, what brings you by?" He motioned to the chair across from his desk. Shuller caught sight of Susan peering through the open door from her desk. As Jeanie took her seat, Shuller crossed over to the door. He shot a cheeky grin to Susan as he closed the door. *That'll keep her stewing for a while. I'm sure I'll pay for that later, too.*

"The boys at the firehouse asked me to extend an invite to you and your guys for our annual cook out in the park. The Fourth of July is only weeks off already. The guys wanted to make sure the boys in blue would be in attendance."

"Are you kidding? We wouldn't miss it. Between John's chili and Jim's smoked pork, mmm, man I can almost taste it now." Shuller perched on the edge of his desk facing Jeanie.

"Good. I'll let the chief know. Do you think we can count on the boys' participation as well?" Jeanie egged Shuller on.

"I'm sure we can twist Frank's wife's arm to get some desserts donated from the diner. But I suspect you're really referring to our annual softball game." There had been a long-standing friendly rivalry between the firehouse and the police station when it came to the annual softball game. "My boys need redemption. Your guys beat us the last two years. This is our year; just you wait and see. We almost had you guys last year," Shuller said. The firehouse won last year's battle in the last play of the game. "We were rallying back up until that triple. It's our year I tell you, you'll see."

"I'll be sure to let the chief know that, too." She smirked.

"Ye of little faith," he jested. Both fell quiet for a moment. Before the silence could grow awkward, Shuller decided to take a chance. He felt he had the home field advantage and took it. "So, Chief sent you over here to make sure we'd participate in the annual cook out, like we have every year prior?"

"Well, you guys may have decided to give up the ghost, being beat the last two years." She giggled. "Then again, it may also have something to do with me offering to walk over to extend the invite personally." Jeanie blushed slighted at the admission. She fixated on a small stray string from the bottom of her blouse.

"Oh, no, we will battle back. And for the record, I'm glad you offered to risk life and limb to traverse the wild tundra that is the parking lot to come visit us here," Shuller retorted. He chuckled a bit and Jeanie returned her gaze toward Shuller and joined in.

"Us?" she muttered under her breath. "*Us*, not so much. You, well that's a different story entirely." Jeanie blushed even more.

PRODIGAL SON

Shuller was taken aback slightly. What happened to the inquisitive reporter from last night? And multiple unrestrained and relentless attempts for information that dominated the latter half of their evening, all gone? Here she was all meek, shy, and unassuming. Was it because she was now on his turf? Had the advantage switched? He understood her brazenness of the night before. To be able to unhinge the person before you by merely being present was intoxicating.

"Despite it being a slow afternoon, I should be heading back to the house. Eventually, I will be missed," Jeanie said slightly befuddled.

She rose from her seat. Shuller stood to meet her. In doing so, they were in very close proximity to each other. He felt a slight low rumble in his stomach. He missed the opportunity last night for the goodnight kiss.

Was this the right time to correct that? I mean, we're in my office for crying aloud, he wondered. Such brazenness was not in his nature. However, the apparent shift in advantage bolstered his resolve. A peck on the cheek, however, that would not corrupt the sanctity of the work place, not even if the workplace in question was his office.

Just a quick one before he can object, Jeanie thought. Although she internalized the same question, her nature took less time to debate the issue and she went for it.

"So I'll let the Chief know we're on then." Jeanie grabbed ahold of Shuller by the elbow and gave him a not-so-quick peck on the cheek. Shuller closed his eyes upon contact. The rough bristle of his budding shadow penetrated her thick lip-gloss. She lingered longer than she had the night before.

Shuller barely had a chance to respond but saw the moment coming. For a split second, he actually entertained the childish idea of turning his head at the last moment. The juvenile rush of a firmly planted peck was thrill enough for the moment. He hoped the subtle presentation of his cheek was not too noticeable.

The fleeting moment gone, Shuller tried to fight the schoolboy smirk from engulfing his face. He walked Jeanie to the frosted paned office door, slipping his arm around her. She certainly did not seem to mind the gesture. As he opened the door, she quickly and discreetly wiped away a bit of gloss from his cheek. While this went unnoticed by the guys in the station, the action did not escape the keen eye of Susan who had been monitoring the door since the instant Shuller closed it.

Jeanie waved to Shuller and then Susan as she left the station. Susan's gaze followed as Jeanie walked by her desk. She took particular note of the girly grin on Jeanie's face as she left. Her eyes shot back to Shuller. Her mouth slightly agape, she gave him a look of surprise. She motioned with a flat opened hand in the direction Jeanie left in as a plea for information. Shuller said nothing as he gave Susan a nod and turned to enter his office. Shuller waited until his back was turned to the snooping secretary before he finally allowed the large smile spill across his face. He returned to his office and closed the door behind him.

Knock. Knock. Knock.

"Suz, I'm not spilling any details, not that there are any to tell," Shuller yelled to the closed door. He was already seated at his desk when the door opened. Shuller had expected to see Susan with her arms folded and a scowl on her face. To his surprise, there stood Frank with a slip of paper.

"Oh, sorry about that Frank," Shuller said. "I thought Susan would have been marching in by now."

"No big deal, boss. I'm half surprised she didn't storm the door," Frank whispered. Frank was more discreet with his notice of Shuller's morning visitor. "Sorry to bother you, but we just got a call in a moment ago. Now, she said not to bother you, but I figured once you heard who called in, you'd want to handle this one yourself."

"Okay, you've got my attention now Frank. What is it? Who called in?"

"Vivian Nash."

The mere thought shook Shuller. He was on instant alert.

"Is everything all right?" His concern was hard to conceal.

"She said she thought someone had been either snooping around her property or spying on her last night. She seemed a bit frazzled–"

"Last night? Why didn't she call in then?" Shuller grumbled.

"I was going to send a guy down to check it out but figured she kind of falls within your purview," Frank continued. "Did you want to go and check it out yourself?"

"Yeah, let me go and check that out now, actually." He turned and snatched his keys off his cabinet and headed out. "It will get me away from the inevitable twenty questions waiting me on the other side of the door," he said nodding in Susan's direction.

"Going out. Possible 10-14, Suz," Shuller shouted over his shoulder to Susan.

"Oh? Where?"

"Viv's. It's probably nothing but going to check it out. I'll call in if anything turns up." Shuller never broke stride on his way out the station doors. *It's probably nothing*, he repeated in his head. This was Vivian after all. *Lord knows what she thinks she saw.* His overprotective nature started to gnaw at him. He hadn't realized how much his pace had quickened as he approached his car. In a blink, he was pulling out of the parking lot and onto Parker Street toward her house.

Shuller pulled into a parking space across the street from the old Victorian. As he left the car, he surveyed the house from the street. He barely took note of the car door closing behind him. He was too preoccupied with checking out the house. A tap of the key fob and a honk later he deposited his keys in his pocket and stood at her front door. He rang the bell. Nothing. Typically, it took her a few moments to reach the door. This time, it felt too long, given the fact she felt the need to call the station. He rested his right hand on the butt of his gun.

Come on Viv.

Then he heard the reassuring scuffle on the other side of the door. Shuller hadn't realized he was holding his breath until that very moment.

"Yes?" she yelled through the door.

"Viv, it's me, Martin. You called the station?" Shuller yelled back. He heard grumbling in response that caused him to raise an eyebrow. He removed his hand from the butt of his gun. Vivian unlocked the door and swung it wide.

"I told them not to bother you with this," she continued her grumble. "It's just the delusions of an old lady most likely."

"Now you know if you're going to call the station for anything, I'm probably going to be the one that comes," he said with a smile. "Well, why don't I come in, and you can fill me in on what you saw."

Shuller stepped inside and headed toward the kitchen. It was practically habit by now. He figured she was making herself some of her tea when she *saw* something out the backdoor.

"So, tell me, what did you see, Viv?"

She shuffled up beside him and pointed out the back window over the sink.

"Over there abouts, by that tree. I saw someone standing there."

"You saw someone standing there. Viv?" Shuller took note of the distance. There was a lot of it between her house and the spot where she pointed. Even midday, it was quite a distance for him; forget about her aging eyesight.

"Don't give me a tone, Martin." She smacked his arm. "He had some binoculars or something. He was looking at my house."

"Are you sure? I mean that is a pretty far distance in the daylight and, to be blunt, you may not have seen things exactly like you think you had late at night," Shuller said in the kindest manner he could muster. He didn't want to come off as disrespectful, not to Vivian.

"I thought of that the first time I seen him out there."

"Whoa, wait. The first time?" Shuller was alarmed. "First of all, how come you never mentioned this to me when I was over here the other day, never mind not calling it in last night when it happened again?" His tone was urgent, but cautious.

"Yes, I know. I wasn't entirely sure the first time, but now I'm certain. I wouldn't call the police for a one off kind of thing, Martin. I've seen him out there before. Now I'm sure of it. Yes, I'm getting on, and I can't make out who it is, but there he stood, in that yard looking over at my house."

Shuller didn't know what to make of what she was telling him. Why would someone be standing off in the distance staring at the back of her house? From where she was pointing, it seemed they were standing on the edge of the tree line in the void between the backyards of the houses that lay between her street and Crescent View Drive. Shuller stood puzzled for a moment. He took a quick look, scanning the area again.

"Let me go over and see what the deal is," he said to her. "Not sure if there is anything over there now, but it's worth a look." Viv nodded as Shuller left through the backdoor. He slowly crossed the backyard to the chipped white paint of the wooden fence that lined her property. Resting his hands on the fence, he looked over to the tree Vivian had pointed. There didn't seem like there would be anything to be found, but Shuller hopped the fence and walked through the void.

The long grass and weeds of the void brushed up against his legs. He continued to stride to the tree. The ground beneath his feet squished beneath his wingtips, much to his dismay. He went trudging through the rest of the rain soaked marsh; Shuller made it to the tree, and thankfully dryer land. He turned and faced Vivian's house. Vivian stood on her back porch to watch him. She waved at him. He stood near the tree and raised his arms seeking confirmation of the suspected voyeur's location. Vivian raised her hand above her head. Shuller took that as an indication he had the right spot.

He scanned the ground looking for anything out of the ordinary. All there was were some random leaves and twigs. There were no footprints as the ground had a firm carpet of grass beneath where he stood. Shuller was aware that, if there was someone watching the house, he could be standing on possible evidence. A quick glance around proved to show nothing. There were no footprints or any other telltale markers that anyone else was ever there. There was a clear cellophane candy wrapper not too far from his now muddied shoes.

Probably blew here randomly, he thought. *What are the odds it has anything to do with what she saw?* Shuller's gut grumbled. He reached in his pocket and grabbed a present latex glove. He bent down and picked up the stray wrapper and pocketed the now balled up glove back into his pocket. He took another quick survey of the scraggly-grassed area and found nothing else out of place. Shuller lifted his shoes and huffed as he looked back at the trek he had to make back to Vivian's house. With a grimace, he trudged back to her yard.

By the time he traversed the void, Vivian had met him in the back as he climbed back over the three-foot wooden fence. He began to wipe the mud off his once spotless shoes onto her grass.

"Well?" she inquired almost immediately as he approached. "I saw that you picked something up, right? Something important, maybe?"

"Viv, I have no idea, but possibly. Or there's a chance it has nothing to do with anything." He tried to assure her, but at the same time, not raise expectations. "It could have been some random trash that blew over the yards. There's no way of telling, but I'd be remiss if I didn't collect anything out of place. I'll bring this back to the station and log it. You never know."

PRODIGAL SON

Chapter Five

Levi scrubbed his hands with the pumice soap to remove the grime of the last oil change. He noticed how the definition of his fingerprints started to ebb away, adding to the muddy brown water capped with white billows of soapsuds slowly disappearing down the drain. The guys behind him gathered stray tools from the various work bays. The clanking metal of the tools was soon masked by the thundering roll of the metal door being pulled down closing off bay two from the street.

"Man, what a long day," Mike said from behind him. He manhandled an oil stained rag as he came up behind Levi.

"Yeah, but a good day. I like the days when we have simple tasks cause you get a lot of them done, but I could have used a tranny rebuild or something."

"Really? Geez, man. Not me." Mike chuckled. He leaned up in the door of bay one. "Give me oil changes all day long."

"Nah. I like digging in and working on a puzzle," Levi said with a smile. He grabbed a paper towel and started to dry his hands. "A challenge is good for the soul every now and again, Mike."

"Good to know. Next challenge that comes in the door, it's all yours!" Mike laughed and Levi joined in.

"You off tomorrow? Got any plans? I was thinking of grilling at the house tomorrow if you're interested. I got plenty of beer," Mike offered.

"I'll have to let you know. I have to head out and check out my grandparents' property. I'm thinking of selling the place. Thing is, I haven't been out there in a while. Shit, 'a while' is putting it mildly. Been damn near ages since I stepped foot on the land. I have to see what condition the place is in, you know. Not really looking forward to it," Levi said with a grimace.

"Oh? I take it your grandparents aren't around."

"They passed years ago. Their property wound up coming to me, and I've kind of let the place go to pot. It's far out in the middle of nowhere, and I don't really get out to the old farm like I should have. It's probably so far gone, I'll have to bull doze the damn thing down just to sell the land."

"Don't get out there much, huh? The cows must be pissed as hell by now," Mike joked.

"You jackass." Levi guffawed. "I sold those along with the other animals and crap when my grandparents passed. I just never did anything about the house and the land."

"They got a lot out there?"

"Nah, not really. Kinda small as far as farms go. I never had the heart to sell it." Levi pitched the used paper towel in the trash as he and Mike started walking to the office.

"Well, just give me a call if you feel like heading over. Just hanging out at the house and relaxing, so I'll be home," Mike said as Levi held the door open for him to pass through.

They stood in the lobby of the shop. Kelly sat behind the counter reconciling the register. She barely took notice of them as they headed to the front door.

PRODIGAL SON

"Good deal, man. I'll give you a call," Levi said. He threw a static wave to Mike and walked out the front door. As he left, he glanced back and saw Mike heading back to the counter, possibly to pester Kelly for some attention. Levi walked alongside the building, headed for the back. He aimed for his car. He fished through his pockets in search of his keys.

Once in his car, Levi slumped in the front seat. He pulled shut the door and sat there for a moment. The thought of heading out to the farmhouse was not going to be the highlight of his day. There was just too much to deal with, and that was just the ghosts hanging around the farmhouse. He let out a heavy sigh and fired up the 'Stang and pulled out of the lot.

As he drove the short distance back home, he mentally readied himself for the only unsettling part of his drive. He turned off Parker and the Mustang roared to life once more. Levi had lasered in on the upcoming light. It was the way he chose to block out *her*. There were days she didn't creep into his brain. Then, there are days that he cannot shake the thought of her. This was a day he was able to block her entirely. It was a welcomed change. Unfortunately, he had only managed to replace his feelings for her with the dread of the next day's dealings. With the six o'clock sun streaming into his windows, Levi made the light and swung a left onto his street riding it all the way around the curve to his house at the end of Crescent View Drive.

He turned off his car after she came to rest in the driveway. Levi fiddled with his keys as he closed the car door. He locked up the car and returned to playing with the overloaded key ring looking for the house key. Somewhere between the car and the kitchen door, Levi realized how tired he really was. His boots felt like they were filled with lead. Home. Sanctuary. He came through the kitchen door and threw his keys on the counter.

He stood and listened to the still of his own house. The only sounds to be heard were the hum of the fridge and the faint tick of some distant clock. He headed to the fridge on autopilot. Levi grabbed a beer off the top shelf. He shut the fridge door and headed to the couch. After settling on the cushions, Levi fumbled with the remote and started surfing through the TV channels. A couple of clicks found some random game and the channel surfing stopped.

Levi sat and drank his beer in the solitude of this living room. The room grew darker as time seemingly progressed without him. He sat, barely taking interest in what was playing before him. The flickering lights of the television and two-thirds of a now discarded beer proved to be very soporific for Levi. He had soon drifted off to sleep, slumped on his couch, still wearing his work clothes.

The early morning pierced the slats of the living room blinds. With almost a planned precision, a ray of light found contact with the face of an unconscious Levi. Bleary eyed and blinking against it, Levi stirred and slowly righted himself on the couch. His aching muscles complained about the choice of bedding, albeit an involuntary sleeping selection. He arched his back seeking a temporary relief from the dull ache, which now engulfed him. He did not find relief. It was just a piece of irony to be marked up and moved on from, a usual happenstance for him. He sighed heavily and slumped over, resting his forearms on his knees.

"This is not how I wanted to start out the day," he complained to the empty room. The declaration was out of exacerbation. He'd much rather be sprawled out on the couch and waiting for that cookout over at Mike's place rather than be dragging ass into the shower and heading out to the old farm.

PRODIGAL SON

Lord knows what that place looks like now, he thought.

He envisioned the house had been reduced to a rundown old shack. He worried it had become a rickety pile of rotting wood; a pathetic reminder of what was once a happy collection of childhood memories. That's what he figured was waiting for him. Not only was the location not a dream destination, it was a long ass drive, too. He grimaced at the idea of driving all the way out there to find what was suspected to be a sad site of a house that once was. He dreaded the trip more than ever since his back ached like that of a ninety-year-old arthritic old man.

Levi had to mentally will himself off the couch and down the hall to his bedroom. As he crossed the threshold to room, his still made bed lay before him. Levi rolled his eyes as he passed it and entered the bathroom. He trudged across the tiles to the tub. He reached into the shower and gave the hot and cold knobs a few hard turns before he started to shed the previous day's clothes. By the time the last item of clothing hit the floor, Levi noticed the steam wafting over the top of the shower curtain. He slid into the shower and turned his aching back into the relentless stream, arching slightly in the hope the heat of the shower would loosen up his shoulders. The water cascaded down his back. He teetered to the side and finally rested his head on the cool titles of the shower wall. There he stood having no desire to move and get on with his day. One of the very few times he didn't wish to move on. He slowly resigned to the pending tasks of the day and reached for the soap.

The morning shower behind him, Levi sat on the edge of his bed tying his boots once again. Slowly plodding through the kitchen, he gathered up his wallet and keys and headed toward the 'Stang. There was little more he needed to collect prior to heading out. It was not a pleasant day trip, after all. This trip was merely an exploration of the old homestead. It would only be to determine if the place was even sellable after all this time. The land, sure, that would be sellable. It was that house, their poor old house. He was already determining that what he would ultimately have to do is get it knocked down and sell the whole lot just for the land. Levi locked up the house and headed to his car.

"I knew I should not have waxed you the other day," he muttered as he settled behind the wheel. "Now you're just going to get all dusted up."

Levi stalled. He sat behind the wheel of his car. The faint *tink* of his keys swaying in the ignition was all he heard. He tilted his head back onto the headrest and closed his eyes. It was not so much the old house or the state he knew it to be in, really. It was the memories, or rather the ghosts, that clung to the old dilapidated house that he didn't care to run into. While he was young, he had fond memories of the farm, his grandparents. So much had changed in his life when his parents were taken from him that one fateful night. He visited his grandparents after his parents had passed, but it was never the same like the trips while they were with him. Nothing was ever the same.

Levi sat up, steadied himself and turned the key in the ignition. *Atta girl*, Levi thought as a smile crept to his lips hearing her engine roar. He put her in gear and eased her out of the driveway. He let out a deep sigh as he approached the light. It was a small victory in his mind that he didn't have to bear passing *her* house again. But his destination didn't make the victory any sweeter; it was just one less cross to bear today.

Soon he was headed toward the highway, past the dusty little neighboring town, the one that was in the papers not so long ago. Levi grimaced as he passed it. His focus soon shifted back to the approaching tarmac of the highway. He clicked on the radio and shifted in his seat, preparing him for the hour or so long drive it was to the old farm. Tom Petty warbled from the speakers.

Finally on the highway, Levi opened her up and cruised north. He would get to see the buildings that made up Tucson set off by the mountains behind them on his way.

His thoughts drifted back to his parents. The ghosts weren't satisfied with waiting for him to arrive. They apparently figured they'd accompany him all the way to the farm. After all, they were lonely, too. It had been a long time since Levi's thoughts drifted their way.

He remembered the excitement he felt when his mom told him they would be visiting her parents for the weekend. They would pack up the car and head out early on a Saturday. Levi would watch the world pass before him from the safety of his backseat window. He would start to see how civilization slowly ebbed away. Soon city life turned to country life, bit by bit. His world changed to this other realm, how brick and mortar gave way to grass and hay bales. He would see how many fields they'd pass with their crops and cattle. It was wondrous for him. This was a world he never knew of before the Swansons.

He was no longer the boy that marveled at what he saw. He was saddened by it. He started with nothing, came from nothing. Levi was bounced from home to home, rather house to house. He hadn't a home until the Swansons. But that was all gone. He frowned at the cycle of it all; from having nothing to being given everything he hoped for, to only then watch it slowly stripped away from him.

This was no longer the journey it used to be. It was not just a long, boring drive. Where it once held wonder to him, it now was nothing but long stretches of nothingness and the cattle he had found fun to count were just *hamburger on the hoof.* With the excitement of his youth long gone, heading out to the farm would be more of a chore.

The morning sun was on its upward ascent by the time he came close to the farm. He saw the exit ahead and kicked over the turn signal.

Why bother, he thought. *Barely a car on the road to care about around here.*

He came to the end of the exit ramp and turned right. The old homestead was just another few miles up the road. Despite the years it truly had been since he ventured to the farm, he remembered the path with little prompting. Within a few minutes, there they were, just passed the grouping of trees, two large wagon wheels flanking a dirt driveway. An old rickety metal mailbox on a pole stood just beyond the second wheel. They seemed to have weathered just fine; he found himself surprised. They had been there probably since God was a child, never mind being there all his known existence. He eased his car onto the drive, navigating between the wagon wheels.

Levi took his foot off the gas. He let his baby idle its way down the drive. Even though he wanted this all over with, he seemed to be in no hurry to get to the house. He felt his gut churn just knowing what lay before him. The car slowly coaxed him down the drive. Trees on either side of him obstructed the view of the house. Soon enough, he breached the clearing.

PRODIGAL SON

Levi's breath hitched as he saw what had become of the place. He jerked the car to a stop. He switched off the ignition and all but staggered from the car. The sound of the car door closing behind him barely registered. The house was as sad as he imagined.

Lord knows what the inside looks like.

The wood shutters were all but corroded away and appeared to be ready to fall off at any moment. All plant life that surrounded the walkway and porch was either dying or already dead. Levi slowly approached the house. He stepped up onto the porch. It creaked beneath his boots. A pungent odor emanated from inside.

As the door creaked open with barely a touch, the musky stench intensified. A wall of webs greeted him as he dared to cross the crumbling threshold. Just past the glass knobbed door, the dense stagnate air carried with it the stench of death, of things gone rotten and decayed. The chandelier was coated in a haze of web, which dangled down in a macabre mane.

The air was gray with dust, caught only by the chards of light slipping past the rips and tares in the thick purple velvet curtains that hung from ceiling and pooled onto the floor. The room was dark. Barely visible were the places where the wallpaper had peeled away long ago. The noise of rats scurrying behind the walls could be heard. At least he hoped it was just rats. Antique furniture littered the rooms, some draped in sheets, and others lay uncovered and faded with time. Levi found it difficult to move about the room. He only managed to stray only slightly from his previous station. The floors squeaked loudly with each step, warning the unwanted they were unwelcomed.

Levi stood in what once was the living room. *Living room.* The irony was not lost on him. It was apparent there had been no living here for practically eons. He slowly scanned around the room, peering down the vacant hallway, surveying each of the walls. Nothing. There was nothing but empty space. Levi stood unable to move. He was as empty as the room. Suddenly, he felt as if he was unable to breathe. Enough was enough. There was no need to damage his psyche any further.

Levi turned and left the house. He didn't even bother closing the door. He suddenly realized he wanted little contact to the abandoned house, whether it physical or emotional. Never breaking stride, he reached his car and climbed in. It was paramount that he leave and soon. He started up the car and threw her into gear. He kicked up dust and debris as he circled in front of the house and aimed back up the drive. He managed to avoid looking at the house as he turned the car around. He was accustomed to diverting his eyes.

God, what a wasted trip, he thought. *What the hell was I thinking?* He was kicking himself, cursing the fact that he had bothered. There was nothing left for him there. There hadn't been anything for him there in some time. *What were you hoping for, huh? Closure? Forgiveness? Not here son. Not anymore.*

He squared his jaw and swallowed hard in an effort to fortify himself from crying. He had himself to blame. The house was not to blame for its state. That was all on him. Levi understood, but still could not bear the guilt of it all and wanted it gone. He stopped at the end of the driveway. He sat stopped between the wagon wheels; he quietly resigned to tearing the place down. *It would be best in order to sell this place,* he thought to himself. Also, it may put to rest the pain, at least he hoped.

The car sat idling. Another bit of irony. He felt that he hadn't moved on despite all of his efforts. He so desperately wanted movement in his life; however, the only movement seemed to be backward.

Levi fumbled for his cell phone. He scrolled through his contacts and found the number he wanted.

"Hey man, trip over?" Mike came booming from his speaker.

"Yeah, just about to head back. That offer still on?" Levi asked, inhaling deeply.

"Oh yeah, beer's chillin' in the fridge right now. Head on over."

"Great. Give me like an hour or so. I'm still at the farm. Gonna take a while to get back to town." Levi drew his lips tight thinking of how to ask what was now swirling around his brain.

"Hey, your cousin, he still works for that wrecking company?"

"Yeah. So thinking of tearing the place down?"

Levi sat silent for a moment. One last thought of the old days crossed his mind. He spurred himself to answer.

"Yeah, yeah. We'll talk about that when I get there. Just make sure those beers are cold," Levi quickly changed the topic as to not dwell.

"No problem, man. Just get your ass over here already."

"K. Heading out now."

He plunged his hand into the ice and water.

"You want another?" Mike yelled over his shoulder. Levi was settled in the lawn chair on his back porch. The chicken and steaks sizzled and popped behind him on the grill.

"Sure. Toss one over here."

Mike pulled out two bottles. He decided better than to throw a bottle at his friend who's already had three thus far. "How about I hand you another? I don't trust you'd catch it."

"What? Can't throw that far?" Levi jested.

"Nah, just don't feel like picking up glass shards out of my grass 'cause your drunken ass can't catch." Levi took the long neck and twisted the cap using the bottom of his shirt. Mike sank into the lawn chair next to his friend. He had positioned his big screen so they could see it through the sliding glass doors, which were propped open wide.

"So Emeril, when's lunch?" Levi pointed toward the grill with the neck of his beer bottle. "Just saying, smelling a bit charred there."

"I guess they could use a turn," Mike said as he clambered from his chair. He strode over to the grill and turned the chicken. Poking at the steaks, he yelled over to Levi, "Medium good for you?"

"Yeah. Sounds great. I'll get the plates."

Mike started piling the steaks on the platter Levi handed him. Next, he stacked the chicken breasts and the roasted corn on the cob on the other platters. Levi carried the steaks to the table while Mike balanced the other two. The two men sat at the weathered picnic table and started filling out their respective plates.

"So, the place as beat up as you thought," Mike asked. He was not sure how touchy Levi was about the subject.

"Yeah. The place was bad. I'm gonna have to hire your cousin to clear it out. The house is a deathtrap. I'm surprised it was still standing from what I saw of it. Granted, I didn't go too far in. I sure as hell didn't try the stairs." He talked about it as if he was retelling a story, not reliving a bad memory. He kept it at an arm's length away out of his own protection.

"Man. Yeah, don't let me forget to give you his number. I'm sure his company can take care of clearing the land for you." Mike could see that the subject was painful. He didn't want to push it much further. It seemed Levi just needed to get some things off his chest.

"I remember running up and down those stairs and my gran yelling that I'd fall and break my neck." Levi chuckled as he popped a piece of steak into his mouth.

"Charming memory man," Mike said, joining in with his own laughter.

"There was something about how it echoed. I remember sounding like a stampede of horses. I thought that was the coolest."

"So, easily entertained as a kid. Stairs, huh?" Mike jested.

"What can I say? I found joy in silly stupid things as a kid." Levi smiled. He realized that he was such a very far distance from that carefree boy. He decided to change the tone before it got any darker. "Oh, you'll love this," Levi swigged a gulp of beer. "There was this one time I was playing out in the barn. Hey, I was an only kid, had to make my own fun," he said as Mike threw him a quizzical look. "Anyway, I was up in the hayloft and I had built a fort out of the smaller bales. I was fighting some epic battle or something, ducking and jumping between the stacks. I got so wrapped up in whatever the hell I was doing that I kind of failed to notice the big ass open window."

"Oh shit, man. Are you kidding me?" Mike almost spat out what he was chewing.

"Nope. I fucking flew out the window. It was cool, for like two seconds, and then fucking gravity took over."

"That must have hurt like hell."

"Luckily for my dumbass there was a cart with some unbaled hay. I fell onto that, but apparently bounced off that and came to a thud in the doorway of the barn."

Mike laughed out loud. Levi joined in between swallows of food and beer.

"I don't remember yelling, but my mom's version had me wailing. I don't doubt it. Broke my arm. Made a great story to the kids in school. I was a regular stunt man."

"Sounds more like a crash test dummy," Mike quipped. He started laughing so hard it prompted a coughing fit.

"Glad I could amuse you. Don't die over it though." Levi started laughing at it as well.

"So Peter Pan, any other attempts to fly or was that the highlight of your stunt man career?" Mike prodded him.

"Are you kidding? My folks and grandparents barely let me out of their sight after that adventure. My life on the farm was pretty mundane after that."

The two guys laughed about that for a bit longer.

"Well, if that's the kind of crap you did on trips to your grandparents, what the hell did you do normally?"

Levi enjoyed the levity for a change. He was able to relax around Mike and not worry about the stupid crap he usually had to worry about. He seemed to have a true friend. Not something he really had much growing up. True, he had friends throughout school, but never that one solid confidant, a right arm, the wingman. He and Mike clicked. They would hang out, catch a game, and shoot the shit.

"Ah geez, let's see. I'm sure I could come up with more blackmail stories for your amusement."

KATHLEEN LOPEZ

PRODIGAL SON

Chapter Six

"Seven then?" Shuller said into the phone. He thought calling would be less nerve racking. He was wrong. He was grateful Jeanie could not see how overly nervous he was at the mere question of dinner and a movie.

"Sounds great. See you then." Shuller could hear the smile on the other end of the line before the goodbyes were exchanged.

It had taken a few more chance conversations before Shuller plucked up the courage to hide behind the receiver of a phone and finally ask the woman on a date. It was that and the constant prodding from Susan day in and day out. Shuller knew he had to hurry up and ask Jeanie out and soon. He didn't want too much time to pass. It looked bad, like he was not interested, if he took too long to ask her. It had been a while since he was in the dating scene, but he had known that much was a universal truth. They had danced around it a few times. It was finally put up or shut up. Besides, Sherlock Holmes sat about fifteen feet from his office door. His internal clock and the looks and questions each time he passed her desk had told him it was time.

Dinner and a movie seemed safe and harmless, he thought.

He wondered briefly if that had become old-fashioned by today's standards; not that he knew what today's standards were, anyway. He left the choice of movie to her. Again, another universal truth he felt was still relevant. He knew this pretty much guaranteed a chick flick, given their first date conversation. He smiled to himself knowing that would most likely be the case. He was fine with that, though. The junior high nerves started creeping up once more.

Shuller faced another problem. It was only two pm. That was a long ways off from seven pm. That was a lot of dodging Susan and her never-ending questions. Not that he prayed for a problem, but something to break loose would be great. He just needed to kill a few hours before he left for the day. He needed out of the office. Otherwise, Susie Q would find any and every reason to come in and quiz him.

Before he made the phone call, he asked Danny into his office to make sure he had the evening covered. Danny had done a great job while he was gone. And he wanted the extra shifts, so it was a no-brainer for Shuller. He chuckled to himself. Here he was lining up someone to cover his job while he went out on a date. This was out of character for him. Part of him felt as if he was shirking his duty as an officer. Part of him didn't care. It's like Suzie Q told him repeatedly, he never took time for himself. It was about time he did for a change.

Just then, a light wrapping came from his office door. Shuller groaned out loud. *Please don't let it be Suzie,* he thought.

"Yeah," he yelled as he gathered some random papers on his desk. It was something to do to hide the fact that he was indeed daydreaming about later this evening.

The door opened and there, as expected, stood Susan. She had noticed his phone line light up and her eye caught the digital readout. She lit up herself when she saw Jeanie's number scrawled across her phone screen. She eyeballed the blinking light until it went out. It was all she could do not to jump up and go running into his office the second the light switched off. She sat there and counted to twenty, her standard wait time. There she stood in Shuller's doorway.

"Well?" Susan made no pretense as to why she was there. She knew he would be expecting her anyway so why insult either of them.

"Was that really twenty seconds?" Shuller laughed. He also knew that was her standard cadence.

"Yes. Heck, I threw in an extra five for good measure, too. Well? I couldn't help but notice you called Jeanie."

"Well, yes." Shuller stopped short of giving her any answers. If she wanted to pry for more details, she'd have to earn it.

"Oh, for crying out loud, Martin."

"Really? Crying uncle so soon? Where's the sport in that?" Shuller chuckled. He knew he was only biding time though. He sighed and figured he'd end the game early.

"Look, it's just dinner and a movie. That's all."

"That's all. Geez, don't sound so excited about it." She smirked.

"I've got Danny to cover. I'll probably have my phone off tonight."

Susan's smile widened.

"Is there anything actually work related, or were you just looking for a little gossip?"

"Just the gossip." She chuckled. She stood there, happy to get some details, but felt that she was still missing the good stuff. For that, she would have to wait. Besides, the real good details were yet to come. And for those, she'd most likely have to call Jeanie.

"Suz?"

"Yeah, well, I'll leave you to it then. I'm going to want details."

"And I'm sure between me and Jeanie you'll get the story you want." He figured that was her plan. He contemplated taking the day off to avoid the battering he would be taking, but that would only infuriate her and surely would not stop her. He smiled at the thought.

"Well, if you want me to handle the details of tonight, oh, and get some work done--" He trailed off.

"Hmm, okay." Susan slowly removed herself from the doorway and returned to her desk.

The fact of the matter was there were a few more details to button up before he met Jeanie. Dinner would probably be the diner again. If this goes well tonight, then next time would have to be a nice restaurant, which meant reservations. He found himself thinking that if things *did* keep progressing the way they had, he'd be like all the other guys in the office. He would see them pass along the "could you order flowers for my wife" tasks to the various admins in the office. He was getting ahead of himself, however. He had to first get the ball rolling.

Man, am I even thinking of that? he pondered. It was another variance of his typical character but another welcome change.

Full and feeling a slight buzz, Levi took another beer from his fridge. He hung over at Mike's for a bit and had some good food with some good company. The meal and game over, he headed home to reclaim some of his lost morning at the farm. He decided to nurture the buzz he started at Mike's. He had a few beers in the fridge so he rationed himself to keep the feeling going. Levi figured he'd kill the few remaining brain cells that maintained the image of the old house and to chase away the few ghosts he managed to stir.

He planted himself in his backyard. He marveled at how sparse the yard was, in fact. There was plenty of space, but he had no idea what to do. Maybe a nicer patio set than the few random chairs he already had or a nice built in grill.

That would look great over there, he thought.

His thoughts trailed off. The ghosts were restless. They wanted, hell, demanded attention. They decided to take revenge on Levi for abandoning them so long ago. They started to stir all types of memories and images in his drunken state. There were things that he hadn't dreamed of thinking about. The ghosts were not satisfied and wanted to torment him some more.

Levi sat in his sagging lawn chair staring around his backyard and then he caught sight of it. His stomach tightened as his eyes lay upon it. *Her* house. God, how on Earth did he find a house that was in the shadow of her house? He had thought he escaped all the shadows of his past. But he was still in the shadows. It made it harder to rid himself of it; the nagging thought of it, of her. There it was every day. Of all the luck, he had this slow torture to deal with every day of his life. He could not even escape at his own home. Levi downed the last of his beer and turned to head back inside.

Levi pitched the empty bottle in the recycle bin outside the sliding door before entering into the house. He grumbled to himself all the way to the fridge. He snagged another beer and twisted the cap swiftly. Levi raised the long neck to his lips and skipped the cap toward the trash. He didn't care that he missed it by a mile.

He guzzled some beer as he leered out the window. The mere thought of her irritated him. She hadn't tried contacting him; in fact, she'd never tried to contact him ever. Why did it bother him, he wondered. It was the never knowing, the lack of rationale, lack of feeling, he figured. There was never a why. Never a thought as to why his life turned out the way it did. He spent most of his young life feeling unwanted. Years of forced solitude. It was slowly bubbling to the surface. He had suppressed it so long, the not knowing, that it was slowly eating at him.

Levi took another long swig. He managed to guzzle half of his beer already. He stood in his kitchen for what seemed like hours, staring. He barely noticed how the light slowly dimmed with the oncoming sunset. He added his latest empty conquest to the growing pile of glass corpses in the recycle bin. The world seemed to be a second or two off sync. He was fully engulfed in a drunken haze. He stumbled over to the kitchen table and clumsily dragged a chair out to sit. Gravity worked double to pull him into the seat. He sat and stewed.

The thoughts that flooded him were jumbled and confused. There was an urgent need to go and do, but go and do what, he had no idea. What was there that he was meant to do?

Then, one idea broke through the fog, *Go see if she ever cared.*

Levi sat and started to string together the disjointed thoughts and images from various parts of his mind.

There has to be some record, some trace of him, right, he rationalized. *No one just walks away like that, do they? What person just walks away and leaves an innocent baby?*

PRODIGAL SON

Seven came way too quickly for Shuller. He found himself all jittery as he drove over to Jeanie's house.

It was a simple diner and a movie thing, right?

Shuller arrived promptly at her door. He took a deep breath and smoothed out his shirt before he reached for the doorbell.

Jeanie jumped at the sound of her own doorbell. She was sitting in the living, in between pacing, awaiting his arrival. She wondered why she was so nervous. Then she wondered if he was as well. She took a calming breath. She didn't want to bolt to the door and seem too anxious. A quick count to ten and then she moved toward the door. As she grabbed the doorknob, she took another deep breath.

Smile, two, three, four.

"Hi, Marty. Don't you look handsome," she quipped and gave the nervous sheriff the once over.

Handsome? Hmm.

"Well, I have to step up my game if I'm to keep up with my present company," he tried for a sly retort. It seemed to have worked as he saw the shy smile spread across her face. "Do you want to catch the earlier showing? Figured we'd head out to the movies first so we won't feel rushed through dinner."

"Sounds fine," she said. "Let me grab my purse." She left him hanging in the doorway while she returned swiftly to the living room.

He took advantage of the few moments she was gone to do his cop thing, peer around and take in the surrounds briefly. He was able to pull back and avoid being caught snooping just as she returned.

"Ready?"

He gave a quick nod and stepped back. She fumbled with her keys as she locked up the front door. The action was not lost on Shuller. He wondered if that meant she was as nervous as he was. *This is our second date after all*, he thought. *Why are we nervous?*

He held his hand out to her and she coyly slipped hers into his grasp. Shuller led her down the path to the street and his awaiting car. The movie theatre was not but a few minutes away, but the way his stomach was tensing, it felt like it was going to be a long, slow drive. Jeanie safely deposited in the passenger side, Shuller closed the door and circled over to the driver's side. All the while, he was internally chastising himself for his unrelenting nerves. He hoped it didn't appear written across his face. As he sat behind the wheel, Jeanie gave him that shy smile of hers as she dipped her eyes from him to the highly interesting floorboards of his car. Shuller smiled back, started the car, and slipped it into gear.

Levi decided upon a more direct route in his drunken haze to get to her house. He decided to cross the void. He strode confidently, or as confident as one could several beers in, to his back fence. He attempted to make a quick hop over his chain link and was suddenly grateful that he had the cover of night to hide the less than successful attempt. Clamoring up from the flat of his back on the opposite side of the fence, he quickly righted himself and made a beeline for her backyard.

His head darted around to see if anyone was watching. While he thought to do so, he never really focused on his surroundings so the act became irrelevant, as his inebriated state didn't give him much time to actually scan the area. He made quick strides across the void between their houses and arrived at the wooden fence. He stopped cold. Merely a foot away, he suddenly felt the urge to use caution. He laid his hand on a slat of the low wooden fence. He stood there peering up at her house for what seemed like hours, when, in fact, it was mere seconds.

"No lights," he said in a whisper. "Wonder if she is out or just sleeping."

What if she was home, he wondered. *What then? Do I confront her? Would she even know it was* me? His plan started to unravel. Why was he standing there? What was the point?

Levi audibly sighed. His gaze dropped to the grass that lay out before him.

This was stupid, he thought. *What would she have that would make anything better? Probably didn't even bother to look at me when I was born, nonetheless keep anything. There was nothing to keep*, he rationalized.

He turned around and started back the way he came, returning to his house.

Shuller held the tub of popcorn and a soda as he walked next to Jeanie to their theatre. She took a drink from her soda as they rounded the corner.

"Number five, over there," she pointed as their theatre came into view.

"Lead on," he said, motioning with the tub in his hands. He let her pick out the seats once inside. She gravitated to the front row of the middle section. The theatre only had a few people occupying the room. The movie was not scheduled to start for another five or ten minutes. Making their way to the middle of the row, Jeanie sat down and Shuller followed suit. He positioned the tub of popcorn between them.

"Thanks for indulging me with this," she said, suddenly breaking the silence.

"No problem," he said with a chuckle. "I'm sure I'm not the only guy in the room here on their own accord."

"It's not going to be that bad of a movie," she scoffed.

"It's the quintessential definition of a chick flick," he replied. The movie theatre was known to have one theatre dedicated to running second run movies. The summer series started with *The Notebook*.

"Aw, you'll love it," she smiled, "or at least fake it for me." Jeanie battered her eyes in an exaggerated fashion.

He opted not to respond and just returned a smile and a simple closed-lipped laugh.

"See? You're good at that."

They both chuckled. Shuller glanced around taking in the fact that people were starting to filter in a steady stream. Pretty much, it was couple's night in theatre five. Many a boyfriend or husband was found trailing their significant other to a seat. Shuller smiled to himself realizing this may be his new reality.

PRODIGAL SON

Jeanie had already started in on the popcorn. Shuller found himself eating popcorn even before the trailers had started. They engaged in idle chitchat when someone a few rows up caught his eye. The telltale glow of a cellphone screen reminded him of his own phone in his pocket. Ever the courteous patron, Shuller dug his phone from his pocket and promptly turned it off. As it was powering down, he wondered why he hadn't just put it on silent.

No difference I suppose. He shrugged and replaced his cell phone in his back pocket. Once he was done, he noticed that Jeanie was turning off her phone as well.

The lights started to dim and the trailers started to roll. Both simultaneously snuggled into their seats, Jeanie with the tub of popcorn in her lap. She and Shuller would make blind grabs for the popcorn as they quietly discussed each preview.

"That one looks good" and "can't wait for that" was shared between the two. Both Jeanie and Shuller silently noted they felt the same regarding the upcoming movies. Perhaps there were more nights like this in their future.

Shuller quietly was aware they seemed to be huddled close together in their seats. He found it amusing that if this is how they would start even before the movie started, knowing how the movie progressed; he wondered how close they would be by the evitable sad conclusion. He could not suppress the smile that crossed his face.

The lights dimmed further. He saw that Jeanie got further settled in her seat. He huffed a quiet chuckle and figured might as well make *the move*. He adjusted in his seat and moved his arm around the back of her chair. She instinctively snuggled into his embrace as his hand came to rest on her shoulder. He could tell from how the screen illuminated her face that she was smiling. At this point, so was he. They both turned to each other briefly and smiled. They focused back to the screen as the movie began.

Levi's pent up anger seemed to have subsided. He turned heel and headed home. He had only gotten a few steps when he heard something behind him. He stopped once more and twisted his head to the side to listen. He figured he had heard a window slide open. He slowly looked to see the soft amber glow of a light from the second story window. *Her bedroom?* The cool breeze of the evening started to ruffle the lace curtains that hung just inside. She *was* home after all. Perhaps that was better. He already talked himself out of finding any physical evidence of his existence in the house, but if she was home, then he may indeed have a reason for a visit. He could ask her why she threw him away. Levi turned back, his anger renewed, and successfully landed a single-handed hurdle over her fence.

He approached her porch and tried the door before him. It was locked. Not one to know how to pick a lock, Levi pondered his options. From his vantage point, he could see into the neighbor's backyard. A baseball bat was lying there close to the fence. He trotted down the few steps of the patio, reached through the slots, and retrieved the bat. He griped it firmly as if he was next up to the plate. He returned to the backdoor with bat in hand.

He tried to work out how to use the bat to open the door. If he broke the glass, she'd be on the phone quicker than he could get to her, so that was not much of an option. He looked up at the door and realized the glass window was a sliding windowpane.

What are the odds, he thought.

PRODIGAL SON

He gave the window a push and it slid slowly, groaning as it slid, as it hadn't been opened in years. It opened enough he could push through the ancient screen, wrench his arm around, and unlock the backdoor.

A quick flick of his finger and the deadbolt slid open. Levi pulled his hand back through the window and slowly let himself inside. His alcohol-fueled anger boiled under the surface. He was mindful to keep it in check as he entered her kitchen. He made his way gradually through the kitchen into what he figured was the living room. He looked around and reviewed the room from what little light seeped through the curtain-clad windows. He saw a little old lady's house. Knick-knacks everywhere, the folded afghan blanket on the sofa. There was not much more than the stereotypical trappings of grandma's house.

Not much of an inheritance, he mused to himself.

He continued his slow creep through her house. He came up on the foyer. The streetlamp had cast a shadow from the front windows down the narrow hallway. He crossed over to a small table with a few frames. He picked up one or two.

"Guess that's dear old dad," he muttered. He replaced them where he found them. He heard a scuffling sound from upstairs. He came around to the foot of the stairs. He stood there momentarily. He was not sure where she was in the house but assumed she was turning in for the night. He saw the light from what he thought was her bedroom bathe the hallway. He took a breath, adjusted his grip on the bat and headed upstairs.

He went extremely slowly up the stairs. He assumed that the stairs would creak and give him away. Unfortunately, for her, they did not. Solid as an oak. He treaded up step by step, his back to the wall. He tried to peer down the hall toward the room with the light on. He had assumed she was in for the evening. As he got within three steps from the top, he realized the scuffling sound he heard earlier was her moving about, out of her room. He came to this realization as he saw something from the corner of his eye. He froze for yet another time and glided his eyes from the doorway down the hall to the little woman to his left. There she stood in the hallway, holding a gun on him that was practically as old as she was.

"You can't tell me that didn't make you a bit sad." Jeanie tried to coax Shuller to admit he liked the movie, deep down.

"Yes. Okay. It made me a little sad," he said begrudgingly.

"Ah-ha!"

"It made me sad that I sat through the whole thing. You didn't let me finish," he quipped.

Jeanie gave him a playful swat to his arm. "Oh please. Well, it's a nice story."

"A nice story? The old lady had no clue what was going on. That's depressing, if you really think about it." Shuller chuckled.

"You're such a guy," she replied with a smile and a shake of her head.

"That's one way to give up a losing battle."

Jeanie mocked shock at his last comment, but followed it with a laugh. They reached the diner as they again decided to take a stroll.

PRODIGAL SON

Well, here we are once again," Shuller said as he reached for the diner's door. "Next time, I should take you to a restaurant in town." The words escaped him before he could really think about what he was implying. *Next time.* He had already become used to the idea. Jeanie smiled as she passed him.

"Well certainly, you'll need to make up for that last comment. A fancy restaurant would be a good start," she smirked as she entered the diner.

"Whoa, fancy? Who said anything about fancy? McDonalds is considered a restaurant, you know. It's in the name."

Shuller continued to tease Jeanie as he followed her into the diner. They were greeted by Terry. Shuller already had geared himself up for the look he knew they were going to receive. Terry did not disappoint. The barely contained amusement that crossed her face told him he would hear about this from Frank in the morning.

"Well, this is becoming a thing with you two," Terry said as she grabbed two menus. "Your usual booth?" Terry smiled as she led them to the booth along the windows. Shuller followed Jeanie, shaking his head. Terry motioned to the booth and the two took to their seats across from each other. Shuller had to shift his phone in his pocket as he sat. It dawned on him that he hadn't turned on his phone since the movies. He thought to turn it on briefly, but figured whatever came up Danny could handle it. He pushed the idea out of his head.

"So, what can I get you to drink?" Terry asked as the two settled in the booth.

"I'll have Coke, Terry. Marty?"

"Sounds good. Make it two."

"Need to hear what the pie selections are or will you need a minute?" Terry still wore the smirk on her face.

"We'll need a minute, Terry," Shuller smiled at her. Terry took her leave as they picked up their menus.

"You've been the one staring at my house," she said. Her voice was not as firm as she would have liked, but it would have to do. At this point, she still had the upper hand. Here he was drunk to the point she could smell it emanate off him holding a mere bat and she had a loaded gun aimed directly at his chest. She had gone to the window to pull in the curtains that had been sucked out by the night breeze when she saw a figure hanging off her backdoor. Her first instinct was to go for her husband's old gun. She scurried down the hall and got it out of the hall closet. She scampered to the phone in the spare bedroom and dialed quickly before she caught something out in the hallway through the open bedroom door. That is when she saw him creeping up the stairs.

"Well?" she persisted. "It's been you, hasn't it? Why?" She edged closer to her room. Hoping he would not try anything while she had that gun on him.

Levi smirked. He arms dropped to his sides. "Well, look at Annie Oakley here."

Despite the gun, Levi took the next step. He caught the fact that the gun shook, ever so slightly. He knew he had her.

"You were going to shoot me? Guess that is the nature of things. Since you didn't give a damn about me before, what's the big fucking difference now?"

PRODIGAL SON

Viv stood confused. She had no idea who this man was before her. She had no idea what he meant. Levi saw it scrawled across her face. He started to laugh. He took another step. Viv shuffled back a step, the gun's vibration giving away her obvious fear.

"Oh, that's right," Levi continued. "Out of sight, out of mind. You threw me away and never gave me another thought. You never once tried to find me, to see how I turned out, if I turned out. You dumped me and moved on," he said wildly. His arms flailed about him. His voice began to bounce off the walls.

Vivian's fear was almost crippling as he topped the last step.

"Now here you are, holding a gun on your baby boy. What a way to say *Welcome Home Son!*"

Vivian's eyes widened. The thought had barely dawned on her as who he was from town, but the realization of what he was referring to hit her hard. She stood there, her mouth agape. The gun suddenly became heavy and her arms could no longer support it. Despite looking directly at him the whole time, when he took the opportunity to lunge forward, she was startled.

Levi took the moment of shock to snatch the gun in one swoop. Upon realizing what just occurred, Vivian let out a squawk and made a dash for her room. Her age and state of being betrayed her when it came to her ability to quickly flee. However, in Levi's drunken state, he felt the need to toy with her. Once securing the gun, he merely watched her scurry away. He took long, lumbering steps in her general direction. The bat was clutched in his right hand, the gun dangled from his left. He chuckled as he hastened his pace slightly as she reached her door. He didn't want to give her the idea that she could actually lock him out, no, not anymore.

Vivian tried to close the door, but it only bounced back open. Levi had stomped his work boot in the doorway preventing her from slamming the door on him. She cowered as best she could against her bed. Levi skulked toward her. He hadn't really thought of what he was going to do. He had her terrified and that soothed some of his demons, but then what? Surely, she would go to the cops.

Hell, the town's sheriff was more of a son to her than he had ever been, he thought. He knew if he just walked away, the cops would be waiting for him on his front door.

She would call the cops on me. She threw me away, and then she'd have me locked away, he thought. He stared her down, seething.

Vivian sank to the floor slowly the closer he got. It all seemed like slow motion. She felt the metal pulls of her nightstand graze her arm as she reached the floor. Wedged between her bed and her nightstand, she looked up at Levi in fear.

He enjoyed the power he had over her, but what to do with her?

"Want to call your golden boy, don't you?" he spat. The rage built again. "You care for *him.* You were married. You seem to be capable of caring, when it suited you. What happened, *Mom?* Was I too much for you? Did I cramp your style?"

Vivian sat and shook. Her voice failed her at first. "We never planned on having children. I wasn't supposed to be able to--"

"Oh, so unplanned and unwanted. Soooo much better," he screamed.

She could not control her tremors.

"I knew some other family could give the boy a better life, but why--"

"A better life?" he cut her off. "Do you know where I spent most of my life? Do you even care? An orphanage. A dank, rundown old orphanage; run by a woman who'd sell you to the highest bidder. Oh, but what the hell did you care? You never *planned* on having any kids anyway."

Levi paced briskly back and forth in front of her. Vivian watched, never once moving from her position. Her hands stayed frozen in midair before her. Levi heaved and continued to pace. He took all the thoughts of abandonment and betrayal and funneled them to aim directly at the woman crumbled on the floor. His father was long since passed, so she would have to receive the full impact of his lost youth.

"Now, here we are," Levi said, raising the gun. He looked at it and laughed. He heard a faint gasp from the frightened form on the floor. His gaze turned back to her.

"Oh, don't worry," he said as he tucked the gun in his waistband. "This," he motioned between the two of them, "this should be a bit more personal, don't you think?"

Vivian stared back. Her head tilted as she gazed back in confusion.

He paused for a moment. He hadn't realized just when he had griped the bat with both hands. He stood in front of her and squared off his shoulders, braced himself by widening his stance. He slowly raised the bat above his head. The strained cries from the terrified woman before him became less and less. All Levi could hear was his own heartbeat in his ears; the crescendo of rushing wind building and building. Then, silence.

Now.

He brought the bat down with his full force. The hollow crack of the wood once it made contact with her skull echoed. Vivian groaned. He saw her arms shoot up and flail. He raised the bat once more and again delivered a swift blow. The sound this hit made was not as crisp as the first. The contact was not as solid as there was already blood and broken bone at the point of impact.

Levi quickened his strikes. Harder. Faster. He rained down blow after blow onto the body below him. Each upward thrust sprayed the ceiling and walls with her blood. Levi lost count of how many times he hit her. The muted screaming stopped. He raised the bat once more above his head and stopped abruptly. He was panting. He surveyed what lay before him. Her face was unrecognizable. Remaining in his position, he rotated his head from side to side and took in the whole scene before him. Blood was everywhere. It covered the bedspread, the walls, his pants, and boots.

He dropped his arms to his sides. The bat was slick with her blood. He heard the clank as the bat hit the floor and began to roll from him.

Leave.

He slowly backed up from where he was standing. He was suddenly sober. He thought quickly about leaving shoe prints, but figured if he just smeared them, the cops would not be any wiser. Besides, he had already mentally decided to burn his clothes and boots in the barrel behind his house.

PRODIGAL SON

He did a quick mental rundown of things. He tried to remember everything he touched. He took the gun from his waistband and wiped it down with the edge of his shirt. He let it drop to the floor by her beaten body. It was her gun anyway. There was no connection to him. He slid his feet down the hall to ensure there were no clear prints left behind as his boots had a considerable amount of blood on them. He made sure he didn't touch the handrail as he avoided it on the way up the stairs. When he got to the foyer, he remembered the photo frame. He grabbed a tissue from the box conveniently on the edge of the table and wiped down the frame. He didn't care if her blood got on it; he just wanted to make sure his fingerprints were gone. He figured there was so much blood on the bat and the way that it slid from his hands, there were no useable fingerprints on that.

He was not sure if what he was doing would help hide evidence or not, but figured it could not hurt. He came upon her kitchen. He grabbed the kitchen towel and wiped down the doorknob and the window. He opened a few drawers and cabinets while holding the towel looking for a garbage bag, something to put his clothes in before he ventured home. He found her stash of trash bags and took one out. He stripped down to his boxers and socks. Everything else went into the bag. He figured the cops might use dogs and follow a trail to his house. He chuckled at the realization he watched too much damned CSI shows.

He left her house the way he came. He tried to put the window back to its original position. Levi ran the towel over the banister just in case he used it coming in. He ran over to the fence where he thought he leaned against to get the bat and gave it a quick once over. He did the same to the small fence that faced the void after he hopped over it for the second time tonight. He put the towel in the bag along with the other items.

Levi was thankful there was not a full moon. It gave him more of a cover of darkness to return to his house. Otherwise, someone may have seen a man running around in his boxers carrying a trash bag.

Levi reached his house in no time. He climbed the fence to get back into his yard. He quickly threw the bag into the burn barrel and quietly replaced the lid. He threw in his muddy socks. No sense trying to wash those. The marshy ground took care of that. He wanted to burn the items, but figured it would look odd if someone started burning anything in the dead of night. He would make it look like he was doing yard work the next day and burn it then. He was sure there would be cops swarming the place, and he'd just be another person finding a reason to stand around and gawk.

Levi crept back to his house after looking around quickly to see if anyone was peering out his or her back windows. Not really seeing anything odd, he went to open the sliding glass door. He took one more look at her house, huffed and entered his. He closed the door, locked it with a smirk, and turned to take a quick shower then head off to bed.

Shuller and Jeanie walked back to the theatre to his car. They were chatting away as they strolled. Jeanie had her hands clasped in the crook of his elbow. They clung close to each other. Shuller was at ease. This time, there was no forced conversation. He found himself dropping his guard.

Jeanie felt like she was floating. She found they would talk and change topics throughout the walk without losing the other. She was happy to have someone that could pick up the changing themes as well as she could. That was certainly another plus for him in her book.

They reached the car, and Shuller opened the door for her.

"Ever the gentleman," Jeanie said, shooting him a genuine smile. She had already buckled herself in by the time Shuller got in and started up the car. The conversation continued to flow all the way home. Not that home was that far away, but it would have felt longer if there were nothing but silence. As they got to the light, Shuller flipped on his left blinker. He instinctively looked over to the right, at Vivian's house, an action not lost to Jeanie.

"I think that's sweet," she said, breaking him out of his gaze.

"What's that?"

"That you think to look over at her house. I think its sweet you check in on her."

"She's all alone; I just think … it makes me feel better to know she's okay. Although, seeing how it's after eleven, I'm pretty sure she's all tucked away in her bed about now."

Jeanie smiled.

The light turned and Shuller continued onto Jeanie's house. A minute or so later, they were parked directly in front of her house. Jeanie undid her belt.

"Oh wait, allow me," he said as he exited the car. Jeanie could not help but let out a chuckle as he rounded the car and opened her door for her in grand fashion.

"Why thank you, sir," she laughed.

He didn't know what possessed him to act so goofy. It felt right so he just went for it. The smile that adorned her face was well worth it. He presented his arm once more, and she gladly accepted it. They walked to the front door, and Jeanie fished for her keys.

"I had a great time tonight," Jeanie said keys firmly in hand.

"Me, too," Shuller replied. He found himself reaching for her hand without realizing it. She didn't protest.

"So next time," he said, his eyes dipping once before continuing, "how *fancy* of a restaurant are we talking?"

Jeanie giggled. "Surprise me. I'd like to see your idea of fancy." The giggles died down and she bit her lip.

They stood there for a moment. The nervous teenager quieted down long enough for Shuller to close the gap between them. Their eyes met briefly. He clasped her hand a bit firmer while his other hand reached for her cheek. He drew her close and their lips met. The kiss was soft at first, gentle. Almost simultaneously, both moved in for more contact. The kiss grew deeper. Shuller's hand slipped from her cheek to the side of her neck. He held her close as she slipped her free hand up his chest. Shuller gently coaxed Jeanie's lips to part slightly. She took a sharp inhale and curled her fingers into his shirt. The kiss was slow as they lingered in each other's arms. Shuller applied firm pressure and then pulled back. He, nor Jeanie, released the other as the kiss ended. Jeanie was flushed. Shuller felt the same. Their foreheads met and they smiled.

"So a fancy restaurant next time then?" she asked after she found her voice.

"Uh huh," was all Shuller could muster in reply.

Jeanie and Shuller slowly relaxed their grips on each other. A few shy glances were exchanged, and Jeanie unlocked her door and slipped inside.

"Goodnight," she said sweetly.

"Night," he replied, unable to hid his grin. The door closed and Shuller inhaled deeply. He turned and headed back to his car. He climbed into the seat where he sat for a moment. As he settled, he became aware of his phone once more. He took it out of his pocket and started to turn it back on. He started the car when he heard the faint sound of sirens. He looked in his rearview as he saw two patrol cars whip around the corner, closely followed by the boys from the firehouse. His phone then chimed. He had several missed calls. Opening his recent list, he saw the station tried calling him recently. He suddenly realized he was still seeing the lights, but no sirens. His chest tightened. He looked back in his mirror and realized they all stopped in front of Vivian's house. Shuller dropped the phone and immediately put the car in drive and made a U-turn and headed over.

The dog was clawing at the backdoor. Vicky figured she'd let him out once more before bed. As she stood on her back porch, she heard a banging sound. She quickly realized it was her next-door neighbor's backdoor swaying in the wind. She found that odd and made her way over to her yard. She left through the gate of her yard and entered Vivian's. She walked up to the door, not thinking anything odd.

Perhaps she didn't close it right, she thought.

"Viv, dear?" she called in to the house. She didn't get a response. She took a step back and realized that the light was on upstairs. She called out again. Nothing. She thought that was odd as well and decided to check on her. She entered the house, calling out to Vivian. She hadn't gotten a response. Her eyes saw a trail of something along the kitchen floor. She could not quite make it out in the dark. *Is that mud?* she wondered. She became more concerned for Vivian and now made her way up to the stairs. The was a dim light from Vivian's rooms which cast shadows down the staircase. Vicky walked up the stairs slowly and encountered an unusual sensation. She smelt something unusual.

As she came off the stairs, her eyes fell to the floor of the hallway.

What is that? she wondered. She tried to ignore the smeared trail of blood.

She called to Vivian again. She was now in the hallway facing the bedroom. Her stomach clenched. Her eyes caught the splatter pattern, but her brain still refused to register it. She kept her eyes straight as she reached the doorway. There was a metallic taste in her mouth that she could not place. Her breathing increased as her brain slowly allowed what she was seeing to process. The utter denial she found herself in was slowly ebbing away. She shifted her eyes to the right and there was Vivian. Vicky's mouth fell open. She wanted to scream, but nothing came. Suddenly, and with great force, Vicky began to scream in earnest. She stumbled in the tracks that led from her bedroom as she scrambled for the phone in the hallway.

"911, what's your emergency?"

"Oh God, oh… you have to… God, oh, God," was all she could stammer.

PRODIGAL SON

"Ma'am? Ma'am, calm down. What is your emergency?"

"Viv…Vivian. It's Vivian Nash. Come. Please. Oh my God! There's so much blood…"

KATHLEEN LOPEZ

Chapter Seven

Soon everyone was out in the streets wondering what was happening down the block. It was hard to miss the squad cars and fire engines that had collected in front of Vivian's house. The rumor mill started in earnest. Soon all the gawkers were talking about how the sweet lady who sat on her porch and waved to passer-bys and never said a harmful word to anyone was murdered. The police tried to keep a tight hold of the details, but it was hard to contain it given the amount of commotion that she simply didn't die in her sleep. It was not hard to determine something had happened other than there being a case of old age or a mere slip in the tub. The story of her death took on a life of its own.

The topic was hours old and was what everyone was respectfully gossiping about, if such a thing exists. Neighbors called friends and before long, Huntersville was abuzz with the sensational story, or at least the one people were creating.

No one could say a bad word about the woman. In all the talk, there were no stories of how she said a cross word to anyone. No one could recount an incident that would lead to an explanation for a crime against her. No one knew the gruesome details, yet. Unfortunately, that would become known, as most things often do. If the town was shocked to hear about 'the who' at the center of the latest crime story, they were in for a wild ride once they hear about 'the how'. 'The why' part was still miles away for anyone at this point, including the police.

The department descended upon her house. The police scoured every inch of the house for any indication of who could have possibly done this to her. Extreme care was taken to preserve any possible trace evidence within the home. The first sweeps performed late that night had revealed quickly that there were smudge marks on the backdoor knob, assumed the point of entry. Despite having very little to go on, the police had assumed that no one would try to enter from the front of the house that faced the busy street.

Shuller was in shock. It had taken a while for him to understand what Danny was telling him. For what seemed like hours, Danny and the other officers would not let him into the house. He was held at bay on the street. He stood shell shocked fresh from his date with Jeanie. He felt dizzy. He anxiously wanted inside the house, but Danny gave orders for him to stay outside. Danny was acting Sheriff and used every bit of his temporary authority. He wanted Shuller to switch into cop-mode before he viewed the crime scene. Even then, Danny worried about how he would react to seeing her in that state.

Upon Danny's direction, Shuller had stopped. It was if he just shut down. Shock must have taken hold of him and he simply stopped. Shuller stood and tried to absorb what was happening.

Jeanie could not help but hear all the commotion just up the street. It was a moment since Shuller left, and she had barely reached her kitchen when she heard the sirens. She went to her front picture window and craned her neck to see the various patrol cars followed by her guys from the firehouse. She saw they were stopping just up the street. She scrambled to put her heels back on, which were discarded once her date was over.

She bolted from her front door and struggled to quickly lock up. Her stomach was in knots. She knew what fire and rescue meant. It was nothing good. She clicked along the street at a quick pace. As she made her way down the street, she started to realize what house they were entering. Her pace quickened. She broke into a brisk trot. She caught sight of Shuller. She saw him being detained by his own men. The few houses that separated hers and Vivian's seemed to grow exponentially as she tried to make her way to the site. She was in a full run.

Shuller never once heard her call for him. He was still processing everything. The next thing he knew, Jeanie was by his side, gripping his arm tightly. She searched his face for an answer. He had felt as if he had missed her question.

"Marty?" she choked out. Out of breath from her run and becoming overrun with emotion, she searched his face for answers. She jerked her head toward the house and watched the boys from the station and firehouse come and go. She raised a hand to her face and turned back to Shuller.

"Oh, no. Please, no." She realized what had happened, or at least she thought she had. She had rationalized that Vivian had died, but she was not sure why Shuller's men would not let him in the house. *What protocol could be keeping him from entering?* she wondered.

It was not until she caught sight of an officer leaving the house removing his latex gloves that she understood the gravity of the situation. She took a sharp inhale and unconsciously held her breath. She swiftly turned to Shuller and saw that he, too, was watching the officer. His eyes tracked him as he made his way to the sidewalk and leaned in to discuss something with Danny. The officer looked distraught. Shuller felt a shiver down his spine and his body visibly shook.

Everything moved in slow motion for Shuller. The sounds that filled the warm night air were muffled and foreign. He felt like he was drowning. He was helpless, especially since he was held back from the activities. He wanted to enter the house; however, the fact that his guys were holding him back terrified him as to what laid inside. What could possibly have happened that they didn't want him to see? His chest constricted with every breath.

Jeanie realized that she hadn't heard Shuller speak since she had arrived beside him. She held tight to his arm with each passing moment. A firm squeeze and a glance up to him got no response. The scene before her and his silence increased her anxiety.

"Marty?" she asked again. She moved closer to him, her arms circled him tight. Shuller never took his gaze off the front door of the house, but moved his arm around her and drew her close. It was his silent way of acknowledging what was happening. He had no words. He knew, as she had assumed, that Vivian was gone. An eeriness about it told him it was not old age that took her. It was not hard to notice that some of the boys avoided eye contact with him, at least not for more than two seconds.

Danny nodded a few times to the officer giving him a quick report. He looked up from the concrete and locked eyes with Shuller. He dreaded what he had to do next. The officer finished his report and gave Danny a tight-lipped look. He moved away, and Danny stood motionless for a moment. He took a deep breath and slowly approached Shuller.

Shuller straightened up as Danny approached. His stomach twisted. The next few moments would be painful.

"Boss," Danny huffed as he finally reached Shuller. "Perhaps you should sit," he continued and pointed to the low brick fence that framed the front yard of Vivian's house.

Shuller's eyes followed his hand, but he remained steadfast and stoic, rooted to the spot where he stood. No other acknowledgement was given to Danny's offer. Shuller braced himself for what he knew was coming. It was not as if he didn't know what all the flurry of activity meant. Jeanie stood alongside him and braced for impact as well. Her grip tightened again.

"Are you sure you can…" Danny trailed off after catching the stern look that Shuller gave him, hard and unyielding. He swallowed hard and continued. "It would appear someone had entered from the rear of the home."

At those words alone Shuller became rigid. There was no way this would end well, but he already knew that. There was no sign of Vivian around, which meant she was still inside. The body language Danny was giving meant that she was unable to be anywhere else but inside. He just didn't know just what happened to her within the house. He reached up and grabbed for Jeanie's hand that was resting on his chest. Her other arm had grasped tight to his hip as she muffled a gasp. She, too, knew the rest of the story would be difficult to hear.

"We suspect then the perpetrator preceded up the stairs and found Ms. Nash in her bedroom."

Ms. Nash, Shuller thought. It was so clinical. That was a bad sign he realized.

"We're not sure why they entered, I mean, there does not seem to be anything missing from the home," Danny continued. "It appears they were alone. There is, so far, nothing to indicate there was more than one other person in the home."

Danny was stalling. He was not sure how to deliver the news of the manner of death. He tried to deliver the facts as if it were just another report. He attempted for a detached or impersonal approach, anything to help the next few words slip from his mouth. He was failing miserably. Danny's voice was on the verge of cracking the more he spoke. Part of the reason was because he didn't know how Shuller would react, and partly because he didn't want to say it aloud either. It was not news he wanted to hear himself, regardless of who said it aloud.

"How?" Shuller's question broke the momentary silence.

Danny gulped air as he swallowed. Something in Shuller broke. The look on Danny's face made him think it was not a simple gunshot. That would be an easier hit, Shuller reckoned, if any of this was to be easy. Tears began to well up in his eyes. The time it took Danny to formulate a response stretched out like eons. He let out a shaky breath.

"Sir, I really think--"

"How?" Shuller barked. His voice broke through the still night air. Everyone within earshot had stopped. All eyes darted to fellow officers, then heads bowed and people shuffled.

"She was beaten." Danny's voice was small. It was all Danny could muster at the time. He hadn't meant to blurt it out like that. Shuller's sharpness had caught him off guard. He drew his lips tight before he finished. "The bat was left in the room beside her on the floor."

Shuller shuttered to a stop. All the air left him. He heard nothing. He stood, wide-eyed. His mouth fell open slightly. *Bat?!* Danny was kind enough not to connect the two ideas, but Shuller's brain put together that someone broke into her home and beat her with a baseball bat. He realized in an instant why the boys refused to let him into the house.

Jeanie tugging on his waist made Shuller come back around. Danny's calls to him went unanswered as he turned to realize Jeanie was curled up in his arms sobbing into his chest. He reached up with his other arm and cradled her head as he pulled her closer to him. He rested his head atop of hers. It was only when his cheek was exposed to her hair that he realized that he, too, was crying.

Danny hung his head. He didn't know what to do or say. He assumed that any minute Shuller would kick into cop mode. He only hoped that Jeanie would keep him at bay just a bit longer. Danny wanted Shuller to absorb the information before he tried to get involved.

"Perhaps you should take her home, boss," Danny attempted, nodding at Jeanie. "The boys have it here. We can brief you in the morning." He hoped that would help distract him. He knew Vivian meant a lot to him. Having him try and work the case right could prove difficult.

Jeanie kept her arm wrapped around Shuller's waist. She knew that he wanted to go, but she knew it would not do him any favors to see her like that. There would be evidence to review soon enough. He would see the crime scene photos that might serve some protection from the brutality of it all.

Shuller was torn. While he wanted to help the investigation, he knew he would be of no use to them. Besides, if the scene was in any way similar to what he only imagined, he didn't think he could take it. In the end, he simply nodded to Danny. He took Jeanie's chin between his fingers and raised her head to meet his gaze. Tight lipped he tilted his head up the street toward her house. She looked up at him and grimaced, nodding slightly in doing so. They turned to leave.

"Danny," Shuller started. His voice sounded foreign and hoarse even to him. "The utmost care, do you understand?" Shuller's point was strong, even though he voice was not at that moment.

"Of course, boss," Danny acknowledged. Danny watched Shuller gradually slip down the street with Jeanie tucked under his arm. He was surprised that he agreed to leave so easily. He was even more surprised that he seemingly handed the case over without a power struggle. Danny got the feeling that Shuller already knew his involvement might hinder the investigation, at least initially. Danny was never more thankful that Jeanie was there. Without her, he assumed there would have been no stopping Shuller from taking over. He was sure that would come soon enough; however, Shuller being in that room that night and looking upon Vivian in such a state would have devastated him.

Shuller and Jeanie leaned against each other as they meandered back to her house. They were in a state of shock. Their footsteps were slow and steady despite the feeling of spinning. The words Danny just said to them were still registering. Jeanie was quietly sobbing, slowly taking in air just to get herself under control. She kept her grip firmly around Shuller's back. Her fingers dung into his hip. Shuller kept returning to that single word repeatedly in his mind. *Bat.* She was such a gentle woman. To be taken in such a merciless manner was mind-boggling.

Despite only being a few houses away, the walk back to Jeanie's seemed to take hours. Shuller listened to the crunch of shoes against the sidewalk. The sound seemed to echo down the street in spite of the activity they just left. He tried to ignore the dancing red and blue lights that emanated from behind him. The sirens had been long silenced, but Shuller still heard them faintly in his head.

As if on autopilot, they reached Jeanie's house and turned up the walk. Neither really looked up, nor at each other. Both of them took on a thirty-mile stare. They only barely registered their surroundings. Jeanie let go of Shuller's arm long enough to unlock the door. She barely remembered clicking the lock as she left her house what seemed like hours ago. Luckily, she had presence of mind to bring along her keys.

Jeanie slipped into the house and Shuller followed behind her silently.

"Kitchen's straight ahead," Jeanie said and motioned down the hall. Her voice was small.

Shuller nodded. He came to a sharp realization that caught him off guard. He physically shuttered at the thought that her house was similarly set up like Vivian's. Shuller trudged toward the kitchen, not registering Jeanie locking the door and following him. Reaching the kitchen, he sat down at the table. Jeanie went straight over to the stove and put on the kettle. She thought tea would be in order. Shuller lifted his head and watched her mechanically go through the motions.

Tea, humph, just like Viv, he thought to himself.

Jeanie turned as if she heard him.

"Coffee in the morning, tea in the evening. Remember?" Jeanie snapped him to the present with the reference to their first "date."

"Makes sense to me," Shuller responded absentmindedly. The smile that teased his lips was gone as soon as it had appeared.

Jeanie took the chair next to Shuller. She looked at him proper for the first time since standing outside Vivian's house.

"I-I just--" she faltered. What was there to say? She clasped her hands on the table.

"I can't even find the words myself," he said. He understood her confusion. He was miring in it himself. He reached up and took her hands in his.

They sat in silence. Jeanie looked down the hall and watched the red and blue lights dance across the lace curtains in her living room's picture window. She suddenly felt Shuller squeeze her hand.

"Jeanie, honey. The kettle," Shuller nodded to the stove.

She was so lost in her thoughts she hadn't heard the faint whistle. She shook her head and rose to take the kettle off. She walked through the steps of dropping two tea bags into the cups and filling them with the water from the kettle. She brought them to the table, forgetting to get the sugar and milk. She returned to her seat, but made no effort to garnish her tea. It sat stoic as she had. She found herself playing with the tea bag unaware that Shuller too made no effort with the tea before him.

"Perhaps I should go, let you get some rest," Shuller suggested, breaking the silence.

"Like I could rest now. Gosh, she was such a sweet little old lady. Who would--" Jeanie didn't want to finish the statement. She sank her head in her hand and rubbed her face.

"Yeah. As much as I want to help the boys," Shuller said motioning behind him, "I don't think I would be any. Hell, it wouldn't help me any to be sure to walk into that."

"Do you think Danny will come down here, you know, to give you an update?"

"Nah." Shuller shook his head. "Don't expect him to. I figure he'll give me a briefing in the morning. Well, later this morning." Shuller corrected himself after getting a look at the wall clock. It was suddenly one thirty-four am. It was if time sped up somehow. *It only seemed like minutes had gone by*, he thought.

"You look beat," Shuller said, returning his gaze toward Jeanie. "Come on," he said rising from his chair.

He extended a hand toward her. She accepted it without a word. He led her to the living room. They left the kitchen with their tea still cooling in their cups on the table. Knowing she was not going to want to go to sleep, at least the pretense of going to bed, he led her to the sofa in the living room.

He kicked off his shoes and sat with his back up wedged in the corner of the arm and back of the couch. Jeanie had followed his example and kicked her heels off to the side. Shuller had settled himself on the couch by having one leg stretched out along the back and one still planted to the floor. He gently pulled her down on to the couch. With little prompting, she instantly curled up onto his chest and he just as swiftly wrapped his arms around her. He brought his other leg up and cradled her on the sofa.

Shuller awkwardly pulled at the curtains as to block the lights filtering into the living room, not that the lace would provide much shielding. Finally successful, he burrowed deeper into the cushions. He tried to ignore the faint hint of the red and blue flashes over his shoulder despite taking one or two peaks out the window. His angle didn't provide much of a view of the activities still going on. He saw a couple of squad cars, but not much more. He figured it was no longer worth the strain it was putting on his neck to look. The outcome was still the same.

Shuller gave up on peering out the window and focused more on Jeanie. He stroked her hair and tugged her closer to him. After a while, he noticed her breathing had slowed to a more rhythmic pattern. He had assumed she had fallen asleep. She had drifted off clutching his shirt in her hands. Shuller dropped his head back into the throw pillows that were behind him and too found some rest.

Neighbors hung in doorways and outside the perimeter of the yellow and black caution tape. All were huddled together, whispering and straining to see what was going on. Danny would much rather they all head inside. They had yet to remove Vivian from the home. The crime scene photos all taken and forensics had completed their job; it was time to remove the body.

The paramedics removed the gurney from their ambulance. From the swell of the chatter around, one would have thought it was some main event.

What did they think they would see? Danny thought. Granted it was human nature, but she would be covered. Danny quickly realized something and jogged over to the paramedics just as they reached the doorway.

"Hey, if at all possible, make sure she is covered well." It sounded so odd to him to even say. "I just want…given that so many are standing around, I don't want her taken out and things to be visible, you know?"

"Yeah. We grabbed extra drapes to make sure there would be *nothing visible* to the crowd." The paramedics were already told it was a particularly bloody scene. They didn't want to carry her out in anything less than a white sheet covering her.

"What a day not to have a body bag stashed in the bus," one paramedic said under his breath as they headed inside.

The paramedics returned to the task at hand. They maneuvered up the stairs and down the hall to her room. They set up the gurney relatively close to her. Both paramedics gave each other a look. They wondered how to get her covered without having blood all over them and the sheet. It was not as if they could lay out a sheet on the floor or the bed for that matter; there was blood everywhere.

One paramedic moved to the gurney and removed the stack of sheets they brought in. He put them on the far side of the bed as that was one of the few places there was no blood. He grabbed two folded sheets off the top and coated the gurney with them. He unfolded them and draped them over the gurney. Looking back at the other paramedic, they had an unspoken agreement. Returning to Vivian, the paramedics flacked her and gingerly lifted her from the floor. An officer behind them skirted the gurney under her as they lifted. It was an added help they needed and both nodded at him in thanks.

They placed her frail body on the sheets and began wrapping her in the flaps, which draped down the sides of the gurney. As they wrapped the first sheet around her, the blood already started to seep through. The paramedics looked at each other again. They continued their work and wrapped the second sheet around her. There was less seepage this time.

"If we strap her like this and wait to put the other sheets over her, chances are no one will see anything. It will by us some time in case there is anything more visual before we get her in the bus," the first paramedic said. His partner agreed.

The second paramedic took the remaining blankets and tucked them under his arm. They wheeled her out and to the stairs. All the officers stopped what they were doing as the paramedics started to leave the house. All of them remained motionless and followed the gurney with their eyes, their heads bowed. The paramedics eased the gurney down the stairs slowly. At the bottom of the stairs, they placed the remaining sheets over her. They nodded to each other once more and crossed the threshold.

There was a thunderous silence. No one gasped; no one spoke. The paramedics rolled the gurney to the sidewalk, lifting it briefly as to get over the curb and into the street. The metallic glancing of the wheels and structure of the gurney creaking were the only sounds echoing through the night air.

They reached the ambulance and guided the gurney into the back. Even though it carried an occupant, the gurney barely felt like it had carried any additional weight. One paramedic climbed into the back and secured the gurney. He reached over and pulled close one of the doors. The other paramedic closed the remaining door. Suddenly and with a whirl, it was as if time unfroze and began again. The random noises of the night coupled with the various activities occurring around the site began as the paramedic climbed into the driver's seat. He flipped on the lights, but kept the sirens off. He slowly pulled away from the scene.

Not only were all her immediate neighbors outside gawking at the scene that was playing out before them, those from the neighborhood in general come out. Some had watched by lining the streets; others simply stood in their backyards and strained to watch the cops from across the void. Police were armed with flashlights as they continued to tape off the perimeter. It was too dark to find really any evidence, but there were a few officers milling around in the back trying to find what they could. The neighbors watched it all unfold. Some were watching with a bit more intensely than others were.

Levi hung in the doorway of the sliding glass door leading to his backyard. He was just like everyone else that night. He was just a regular nosey neighbor. *If I did not hang around and gawk like everyone else, it would look odd*, he thought. He was just watching the police. His eyes followed the cops walking around the backyard, taking photos, sweeping their flashlights across the ground. Levi's eyes jutted between the police and the burn barrel in his backyard. He was glad they were too far away to see the smirk crawl across his face.

His eyes returned to watching the cops. He made a note to get up early and tidy up the backyard and light the debris in the barrel, or to make it look like that was what he was doing. The lid was secure enough for him not to worry about leaving it out in the open. He was cocky in the belief that they had no clue as to what happened given the fact that they were still swarming around the house randomly. If they had something, they would seem to be a bit more focused. He figured if he was out first thing *cleaning his backyard* would look like just another nosey neighbor still finding something to do outside while casually looking over to see what was going on. Besides, the contents in the barrel weren't going to burn themselves.

KATHLEEN LOPEZ

Chapter Eight

The light of next day didn't help illuminate any more details. There were still as many questions, if not more, than they had when they first got the call about Vivian. The station was alive with noise. The phones were ringing off their hooks, people were scurrying about, and the constant murmur of conversation never ceased.

Frank had just put down the phone for what seemed like the tenth time and was scribbling notes when his eyes caught sight of familiar shoes. There Shuller stood, again, just inside the doorway. He felt that if spoke some spell would be broken; it would all become too real. He scanned the room and took in all the activity. Shuller hadn't noticed Frank staring motionless at him.

"Boss?" Frank practically whispered. His voice carried as the whirl of movement behind him slowed. Shuller felt as if the whole station was eyeing him, waiting for a response. The next thing he was aware of was being engulfed by Susan.

"Oh, Martin," she said as she wrapped her arms around him. He groggily raised his arms around her and returned the embrace. She slipped back a bit and looked at him directly. "I'll get Danny to give you the run down in your office. I just put on a fresh pot. I'll bring you some in a minute, okay?"

Shuller just nodded and allowed him to be led to his office. She cast a *get back to work* glare to the milling crowd, and the coordinated efforts of the force resumed.

Shuller planted himself behind his desk. Susan slipped out and went along to get him his coffee just as Danny was entering his office. Shuller took a deep breath and exhaled slowly. He tried to make it not obvious, but Danny had expected it. He paused shortly before he started in.

"I hate to start off this way, but except for a more detailed account, what I told you last night still holds. We don't have much to go on."

"You said that the, uh…bat…was left there. Any prints?" Shuller tried to keep a professional façade in place as the words crossed his lips.

"Nothing forensics could really use. There were prints, but they were too smudged. It doesn't appear he wore gloves. They found a few smudges like those that he went through and wiped down surfaces before he left. We found a gun on the scene registered to Vivian lying next to her. Not sure if she tried to use it or if he did, but it was wiped clean as well. We assumed that at one point he was holding it since he took the time to wipe it."

Shuller nodded and sighed. He saw that Danny was clutching a folder. He knew what that folder contained. Photos. His stomach clenched at the thought. Danny had the evidence reports in that folder along with any photos taken from the crime scene. He was hesitant to ask for the folder, and Danny was hesitant to hand it over.

"So, no note, no threatening phone calls…" Shuller trailed off.

"No. I had the boys pull her phone records to see if there were any reoccurring calls or calls that night. There was nothing outside of her normal circle of contacts. Nothing to indicate she was being harassed." Danny's eyes dropped and he drew his lips together tightly.

"Uh, boss, there was a call placed from her house that night," Danny finally uttered. "The boys found a phone in the room down the hall that was off the hook. We assumed she was interrupted before she returned to her room either by her choice or the intruder."

It became obviously to Shuller that there was something Danny seemed to be holding back. There was a clenching feeling in his stomach. Then it hit him. His phone. He had turned it on, but was distracted by the sirens that night. He never properly looked at all his missed calls or if he had any messages.

Shuller and Danny stared at each other for a moment. Shuller's eyes closed over as he leaned over and fished his phone from his back pocket. He stared down at it for a moment. Lord knows if there was anything there, but if there was, he hoped it would give them some clues as to what happened.

Shuller unlocked his phone and opened to the recent calls. The first few were from the station, just as he saw. Then, there it was – Vivian's call. Shuller felt a lump in his throat. His eyes darted over to the voicemail icon. One. He stared at that red dot until he thought it would burn his eyes. He glanced up at Danny. Danny scooted to the edge of his seat. He dipped his eyes to the phone then back at Shuller. Shuller opened his voicemail, pressed play, and then pressed speaker before putting the phone on the desk between them.

What came over was muffled. The call started with a very sharp static-like sound, the sound of material rustling against the receiver. Shuller shot a confused look at Danny.

"The phone receiver was found on the bed next to the nightstand," he said almost apologetically.

"Great," Shuller huffed. "We probably won't hear a damn thing."

The quilt that the phone was lying on did muffle most of the sounds. They heard faint traces of a conversation. Neither of them raised their voices much during the confrontation.

"They're not yelling?" Danny said puzzled. "Do you think she knew him?" Danny already knew the attack was suspected to be personal given that the bat was preferred over using the gun.

"How could anyone who knew her do that?" Shuller snapped pointing at the phone. "It sounds like a male voice, kinda deep."

"It would almost have to be," Danny started, but held back from finishing his thought. After all, he had seen the result of this confrontation. Both he and Shuller leaned closer to the phone to see if they could make out any more of the conversation. They figured by this point in call, Vivian had moved closer to her room and that both were facing away from the direction of the spare room.

"That may be it. There were no more sounds really registering on the phone. Perhaps forensics can..." Danny was cut off. The sound of Vivian screaming was heard, albeit briefly.

Shuller and Danny righted themselves and instantly felt ill. There were a few blunt sounds then a clank of wood on wood. They figured that was when he dropped the bat. The voicemail recorded a second or so longer before it cut out completely. They sat there stunned.

Neither knew what to say. Shuller sank back into his chair; his eyes never left the phone. Danny stayed motionless.

"Uh," he stammered. He dared a look up at Shuller. "I-I'll see if the techs can, uh, Jesus!" He ran his hand through his short brown hair.

"Yeah. Go ahead and take my phone over to them. Guess they can forward that to whatever. I can't even think." Shuller sat and shook his head. Shuller motioned to the folder that lay slack in Danny's grip. "Before you go, is that for me?"

"Oh. The report from last night, and the preliminaries."

"I would imagine the photos as well?" Shuller ventured when he saw that Danny would not discuss the 800-pound gorilla sitting in the middle of the room.

"Yeah, boss. The photos are in there." Danny slowly placed the folder down and then reached for the phone.

"I'll get this to the techs," Danny said already rising to make his exit. He didn't want to be in the room when Shuller opened that folder. He was uncomfortable enough looking at them the first time; he didn't want to sit there while Shuller viewed them. Besides, he figured Shuller might want to view them in private. It was going to be hard enough to look at them without someone staring at him while he did so.

"I was going to head back over to the house in a few, to see if the guys had any more luck this morning," Danny said and gave him a nod and made a quick exit. He closed the door behind him. He went over to Susan to let her know that he gave Shuller the file.

"I'll run interference to make sure he has some time to digest it. The poor dear," Susan said, looking back at the closed office door.

"Yeah, she didn't deserve that," Danny replied. He griped Shuller's phone and threw a curt smile to Susan as he turned toward the back offices.

"I wasn't just referring to her," she mumbled as Danny walked away.

Shuller stared at the folder. He had no real desire to open it, but as a part of the job, he was compelled to look it over. He leaned across his desk, reaching for the folder as if he was about to pet a rattlesnake. He picked it up and sank back into his chair.

Rather thin, he thought, but there was so little to go on, the folder would barely contain much of anything.

Shuller took a deep breath and opened the folder slowly. His eyes fell to the written report. He honestly only comprehended every other word as the photos to the right were begging for attention. He kept his focus on the reports, which helped blur out the images. Subconsciously he figured that would be best; however, the primary aspect that registered was the color red. Knowing he could not avoid it any longer, Shuller's eyes darted to the image clipped to the folder flap.

The first image was that of the floor. His brain tried to interpret the puddle as melted candle wax pooled around a discarded baseball bat. There was no way that was blood, Vivian's blood. He flipped to another photograph of the blood patterns across the wall, the bed. He then saw Vivian. Well, what he saw was a blood soaked nightgown and her legs. He could not get his eyes to venture further across the photo. Shuller was transfixed to that portion of the image. He knew, from briefly reading and listening to the reports, what the other half of the image could possibly contain. He was concerned he could not handle the reality of it. Shuller was not sure what was worse, the image he created in his head or the photographic evidence that lay before him now. He rolled his eyes shut and took a steadying breath, exhaled, and opened his eyes.

His gaze scanned over the frail body in the photo. Then he saw the full impact of what damage she sustained. It could not have been but a nanosecond or three before Shuller felt the bile at the base of this throat and slammed the folder shut. He threw the folder on his desk as if it burned him. He stood and promptly left his office.

"I need some air, Suz," he said, without much of a look in her direction. His eyes were focused on the front doors.

"Uh-okay," was all she could get in before he was already rounding the front desk and making a beeline to the street.

The poor dear, she thought.

As busy as the police station was, the firehouse was stone silent. The guys on duty milled around like usual. A few played a card game while a television murmured in the background. Occasionally the rustle of the day's newspaper would break the quiet. Of course, the lead story was the previous evening's murder.

"The boys up the street have their hands full with that one," one of the guys motioned to the paper.

"No kidding. I still can't get my head around it. Pauly and I were on call last night, too. Damnedest thing," he said. "I can imagine some of them are feeling it more than others." He nudged his head toward the front office, where Jeanie sat.

It was not much of a secret around the firehouse that Jeanie had started dating the sheriff. The guys figured Jeanie would have the inside track when it came to how Vivian's murder was affecting him. They could not help but notice how she was affected too. Everyone knew she only lived a few doors down from her.

Jeanie had found herself daydreaming during the course of the morning. She drifted off in the quiet moments, which was most of the morning. Her mind kept revisiting the sound of the sirens, the tightening of her chest as she started to run down the street, the shock of the moment she realized what she was witnessing. Jeanie's thoughts drifted toward Shuller. She was wondering how he was coping.

Officers roamed around, talking to neighbors, trying to get some clue as to who or even why someone would bludgeon a lonely woman. A few officers gathered at the back of the house. Forensics was dusting every inch of the railing and fence post; a fact that did not go unnoticed by the watcher from across the void.

Did I wipe down the fence post? he thought. He shrugged and struck the match he was holding in his hand and unceremoniously tossed it into the burn barrel. The lighter fluid soaked materials went up in an instant. The sudden burst of flame caught him off guard. He chuckled slightly. He glanced over the flames to see what the cops were doing. It was all just a part of being a noisy neighbor.

Levi gathered a handful of leaves in his arms. As he turned around about to dump them into the barrel, he noticed a couple of cops had jumped the fence and started to tromp around in the space immediately behind her house. While one cop searched around aimlessly, the other started to traverse the void, in the direction of Levi's house.

PRODIGAL SON

The inbound police officer did little to faze Levi. He dumped the armload of leaves and debris into the flames. He made a mental note that the smoke rising from the barrel smelt of nothing more than dank smoke and lighter fluid. Burning rubber was a concern, but apparently, the ample amount of lighter fluid took care of that, combined with the intensity of the flames. Levi simply returned to clearing up the yard and dumping small clumps of twigs and leaves.

"Hey, there," shouted the cop as he approached Levi.

"Hey."

"Mind if I ask you a few questions?"

"Sure, officer," Levi said, dropping the latest collection of yard debris into the barrel and clapping his hands to rid the dirt from them.

"I am not sure if you are aware or not," he said as he motioned over his shoulder toward Vivian's house.

"The old lady. Yeah, heard about that. Shame. She seemed nice," Levi offered. The words burnt the back of his throat. He tried to push the thought away and keep a calm face as the cop continued.

"Were you home late last night? Say around eleven pm?" the cop asked as he rested his hand on the back fence.

"Yes, actually I was, officer." Levi felt no reason to lie. It was not as if he made any noise or alerted anyone when he left. He would be just like every other neighbor.

"Did you happen to hear anything, or see anyone hanging around the property?"

"No, not really. Kind of a quiet night really." *Except for the screaming,* he kept that detail to himself.

"Did you know Ms. Nash at all, sir?"

"I knew of her, but I didn't really know her, not really. Just kind of heard about her." This was true. He certainly knew of her.

"Alright, if you happen to remember anything about seeing someone hanging around the neighborhood or anything like that, please give us a call at the station," the officer said.

A quick nod was exchanged between the two. The cop glanced down at his muddy shoes with a grimace. He looked as enthused to trek back across the muddy field as Levi was when he had to do it. Levi returned to his yard work as he watched the cop retreat across the void. He tried not to let the smirk on his face creep too wide as he dumped another armload of leaves into the barrel.

Jeanie felt for the poor lady shifting before her. It was not the best timing and Jeanie understood that, but there was so much planning gone into the annual town picnic that it could not be stopped.

"So, uh…" Kelly struggled with finding the right words. "The department is up for participating then?"

"Yes, hun. Chief spoke to the guys this morning and they agreed they would still take part. It's a bad situation, but perhaps we could celebrate her somehow, you know. She certainly wouldn't want the whole town to shy away from the picnic."

"True. She was such a sweetheart. It's just senseless." Kelly stood and shook her head.

"Yeah. Just a sweet lady," she said, almost in a whisper. "Have you spoken to the boys?" Jeanie asked, referring to the police up the street.

"That's my next stop. Do you think they will opt out this year? The annual cook off and ball game between you two are a real draw for the town." Kelly bit her lip. She was concerned that she was still coming off as callous.

"I'm sure the boys would feel the same as my guys. They would do it *for* Viv, not in spite of--" Jeanie trailed off.

"I'm sure. Well," Kelly said, already feeling the weight of it all in the pit of her stomach, "let me go down and check with them. Do you think the sheriff is in or is he … at the house?"

"I'm not sure. He may still be at the station. I think Danny was running this one," Jeanie said with a pained, tight-lipped expression.

Kelly gave her a meek smile and made her way from the office and the firehouse altogether. She needed air quickly as well as distance from the conversation. She took a deep breath as she reached the sidewalk and turned toward the police station. The few yards between the two felt like miles up hill. She felt so tactless to ask, but the town's planning committee had to make sure that they wanted to proceed with the event seeing how it was within days. Kelly worked out the conversation in her head as she walked to the station. She dreaded talking to Shuller to be honest. Everyone knew that Vivian had no family, but he was the closest to her. He was her surrogate son, and here she was going to ask him if he was going to attend a big party days from her brutal murder. Her stomach flopped with each step. Before she realized it, she was halfway up the few steps to the front door.

She entered the station and saw the random commotion. Police officers were fielding calls and talking in groups. It seemed a bit busier than a normal day. Well, it was not just a normal day, was it? She caught Frank's eye as she approached the front desk.

"Hi, Frank." *It sounded a bit apologetic from the get go,* she thought.

"Hey, Kelly, dear. What can I do for you?"

"Gosh, this seems so tacky, but the guys down at City Hall wanted to verify the station's participation for the town picnic." She winced as the question left her lips. "I was told to ask both the firehouse and police station, given your guys involvement in it all. The guys at the fire station said they were participating, kind of in her honor." There was no need for Kelly to clarify whom she meant. "I was not sure how the boys felt, given, well how she and the sheriff were so close. I really hate to ask, and I want to express the staff of town hall truly express their sympathies at this time, but--"

"Kelly, dear, don't hurt yourself," Frank interrupted her. "I'll go check with the boss."

"No need, Frank," Shuller said over his shoulder, startling the front desk clerk in the process.

"Geez, boss, didn't hear you there. Kelly was here asking--" he started as Shuller cut him off.

"I heard. Yes, the station will also honor Viv. Of course we will. Don't think she'd take to kindly if we made everyone work so hard to put this all together and then call it at the end." Shuller tried putting on a brave face. He barely convinced himself. "I'll make sure our boys are there for the town, for Viv."

"Thanks, Sheriff," Kelly exhaled finally. "I'll let the committee know." She gave a brief wave and practically bounded out of the station. She felt a weight lifted from her as soon as she reached outside.

"I'll tell the boys," Frank offered.

"I appreciate that, Frank."

"So are you heading down to the house?" Frank, like everyone else, suddenly had taken issue with saying Vivian's house. They certainly refrained from calling it a crime scene as well.

"Nah. Danny has it covered. Besides, I don't think I could...it would be best for the investigation if I stayed clear a bit. Wouldn't want to mess this up. Too important."

Shuller's eyes glazed over a bit as he stared off. He startled himself out of the self-induced trance. "Let me know if you need anything, Frank. I think I'll head up the street for a visit."

Frank knew exactly where he was heading without Shuller really having to say it.

"I'll hold down the fort, sir."

Shuller winced as the midday sun streamed down. He hadn't realized how cooped up he felt not being involved more. He did realize that he could not sit there waiting for Danny's next report. He was going stir crazy. He had a sinking feeling there would be next to nothing to report anyway.

He turned up the street toward the firehouse, toward Jeanie. He was in no real rush. He needed to take his time. He knew that every time he thought of the case, every time he replayed that voicemail in his head, he would start to breathe harder. He tried to calm himself with long slow breaths. He took long slow strides, thinking he could time his breathing in step. It took a little coordination, he found, but he soon felt a bit more at ease. He still had a bit of a way before he reached the firehouse.

Jeanie had drifted off again. Her mind wondered back to that night. This time it was to the morning after, really. She recalled waking up on the couch, curled up in Shuller's arms. She remembered lying still for a moment trying to get her bearings. She was not accustomed to waking up on her own couch too often.

Once she realized where she was, and why, she remained still. It was a brief denial on her part, hoping that she was just waking from a bad dream. She realized she was not. She slowly started to realize that Shuller was not sleeping. He'd shift minutely, trying not to disturb her. She raised her eyes to catch him flicking the curtains caught in the breeze as it lapped at the back of the couch. She was not sure if had even slept at all. Jeanie tried to remember if he had drifted off before her or not. She was concerned he stayed up all night. She burrowed in a bit and wrapped her free arm tighter around Shuller.

"You awake?" he asked.

"Yeah. Barely. Did you getting any sleep?" She had guessed that he would not tell her if he hadn't slept much.

"A bit, yeah."

Jeanie figured that was possibly true, but she doubted how much "a bit" really was in truth.

Jeanie was snapped back to the present with the gust of warm air that hit her when the front door opened. In walked Shuller. She flashed him a timid smile.

"Just spoke to Kelly. Poor thing looked like she was going to shatter," Shuller said after Jeanie greeted him with a hug.

"Yeah. She was over here checking on our participation before she hit the station. So the boys going to join us?"

"Wouldn't consider backing out. It takes a lot to put this on, so we wouldn't want to disappoint anyone. Besides, it would be a dishonor if we didn't."

Jeanie knew what he meant without pushing it further. Just then, the fire chief approached the two of them.

"Martin. How's things?" he asked gently.

"As well as to be expected," he answered. He really didn't know what else to say.

"Any word?" The chief was being very economical with his words, testing the waters.

"Well, from what Danny said, there is little to find. I don't have much faith we'll catch a break on this one." Shuller tried to stay detached, but he was starting to falter.

"Well, anything you or the boys need, don't hesitate to ask."

"Thanks. We'll see you and your guys in a few days," Shuller said as he pointed across the street to the fields in the park.

"Sure thing," Chief said and nodded as he retreated from the office.

Shuller grabbed a seat across from Jeanie's desk. The fatigue was evident as he sagged into the cushioned seat. Jeanie bit her bottom lip while she considered broaching a topic she was not sure if Shuller could handle at this point. He looked up at her, his eyes hooded.

"What's on your mind?" He was cautious not to use an abrasive tone, despite feeling worn out and frustrated.

"Well," she hesitated slightly, and then continued, "since she had no family, who's going to take care of everything?"

Shuller considered this for a moment. The idea hadn't crossed his mind. Her effects would have to be taken care of, and then there was a service or a funeral to arrange. His eyes widened as he took in a deep breath.

"You know, I hadn't even thought about it. I'm not even sure if she had a will. I can get Suzie Q working on some of that. Between the two of us, we'll get everything sorted for her." He actually felt a bit relieved. This gave him something he could do for her, even if he didn't trust his emotions with the actual handling of the case.

"I'll certainly help where you need a hand," Jeanie offered with a slight smile.

Shuller sat in silence for a moment. He had a contributing task, but the thought of sorting things for Vivian was daunting. He looked up at Jeanie. She fiddled with the pendant on her necklace as she stared at him with concern. It was not an uncomfortable look, Shuller registered. Shuller returned a soft smile. He knew he should head back to the station, but he found a bit of peace just sitting there in the quiet with Jeanie.

PRODIGAL SON

"I should head back," he finally voiced. He didn't like the idea of leaving, but he could not sit there all day, no matter how soothing it felt.

"Well, you are the Sheriff, I'm sure you could get a little slack," she quipped. That got a slight chuckle from the stoic Shuller.

"Quite possibly, but I should head back all the same," he said as he rose from the chair. Jeanie mirrored him.

"Hey," she said as she rounded her desk. Jeanie crossed over to Shuller and simply and slowly wrapped her arms around him. Shuller slumped into her embrace. She moved in cautiously and tilted her head. Her lips brushed his gently as she stopped, as if asking permission. Shuller responded by moving in and claiming her lips. His arms rose to her hips, drawing her in. He inhaled sharply taking in a large dose of her fragrant perfume. She tightened her grip, eliminating the space between them.

Shuller wrapped his arms around Jeanie and held her close. He blocked out everything but her. Shuller was not one for public displays of affection, but at this moment, he didn't care if they were in the center of town. There was no thought to the large windows that opened to the truck bay. Little concerned him at that moment other than Jeanie. He encircled her with his arm while slipping one hand from her back to cradle her face. He clasped her cheek as a small moan escaped her lips. Shuller brushed her cheek with his thumb as he moved his hand to thread his fingers through her hair.

Lips gently battled for dominance between the two. Jeanie curled her fingers into the back of Shuller's dress shirt. It was a matter testing their will to continue with the kiss rather than breaking for desperately needed breath. Finally, the basic necessity of life prevailed and they broke apart. Each clung to each other, panting.

Shuller tilted his head slightly as they rested their foreheads together. He stole a glance out of the corner of his eye out the large panes of glass. Shuller was instantly aware that they were not in some secluded haven. A smirk graced his face as he ascertained they did not have an audience.

Jeanie remained, not wanting to break the spell. Shuller shifted his attentions back to Jeanie. He smiled. Jeanie looked up through her lashes and smiled back.

"Ahem, well," Shuller started, "I really should go." He continued to smile at her as he stepped from her embrace. His reluctance to do so was apparent. Jeanie groaned her disapproval.

"Yes, I suppose you do," she replied and slipped her arms from around him. They parted and Jeanie stepped back and braced herself on the edge of her desk. She gave Shuller a shy smile and dipped her head. Shuller shuffled his stance from side to side.

"So, for someone who is so keen on leaving," she smirked and looked at him directly, "you don't seem to be in a big hurry."

"To be honest, it's not my personal preference, but I am on duty."

"I don't want to deprive the town of its sheriff now. But answer me this before you go. Are you going to be okay, really, I mean for the town picnic? It's a few days off and with everything still going on, I want to make sure you're okay."

Shuller started to step forward, but hesitated. "I'll be fine," he said gruffly. He took in a sharp breath and held it momentarily. "Yeah, I'll be okay," he said exhaling.

"You need anything, you call," she ordered.

"I got it. Thanks. Really heading out now," he said, motioning to her office door. Shuller nodded once and crossed to the door. "You'll accompany me for the town picnic, though?"

"Absolutely," Jeanie said, the smile that fleetingly slipped from her lips had returned.

Shuller allowed a look of gratitude cross his face before he exited her office. He strode across the slick concrete of the fire station bay and out to the street. Shuller turned in direction of the station and adopted a measured stride back to his office.

The days passed uneventfully. Normally that was a blessing, but when in the midst of a murder investigation, it was the worst kind of luck. Danny trudged back to Shuller's office day after day with not much to report. Forensics found little to nothing in the way of trace evidence to assist in any investigation. Shuller didn't know what hurt most, not having any leads or the stress he saw building in Danny.

He would assure Danny each time that he was not to blame; the blame lay with the bastard who committed the crime. Shuller danced a fine line with guilt and anger, but tried to keep it from the boys on the force and focused toward the situation.

Shuller ran his hands over his face. He lay in his bed trying to determine how to play the day. It was the day of the town picnic. Was he to walk around sullen? Were people expecting him to be mournful for Vivian or vengeful? The truth was, he was exasperated at the whole situation. That was certainly not the message to transmit to the town. But what other option had he left? The papers were covering the progress, or lack thereof, of the investigation.

How was he to exhibit any confidence in finding her killer? How was he going to answer the questions he knew were coming his way?

Shuller grunted as his arms dropped to either side. He lay there staring at the ceiling for what seemed like hours. He turned to steal a glance at the alarm clock. Seven forty-five glared back at him in an angry red numbers. He turned back to his gazing at the ceiling before he decided to get out of bed. He rubbed his cheeks and jaw as he schlepped to the bathroom. He heard the scratch of the stubble beneath his hand.

Quick shave and a shower, he thought. Not much of a day's preparation, but it was all he had at his disposal. He went straight to the shower and reached for the knobs. The shower sputtered to life. He grabbed his toothbrush and toothpaste while he waited for the water to be more inhabitable. By the time he turned off the sink, spigot steam billowed from behind the curtain.

Shuller stripped out of his boxers and stepped into the steady stream of hot water. The water cascaded over him. He closed his eyes, raised his head, and took on the water directly. He merely stood there letting the water sheet off him. After a few moments, he reached for the shampoo.

Down at the park, tables were already being set up. The banners were being hung and random activities were going on in preparations for the opening festivities. Jeanie had offered to help with the setup of the various booths around the perimeter of the park. She had arranged to meet Shuller at the park. She had assumed that he was just going to slip into the crowd at some point in the morning, not that he was going to keep his anonymity too long. She assumed there would be a continual run of people coming up to him asking how he was doing and how the investigation was going. People always seem to ask about ongoing investigations only to be told they cannot be told anything. Jeanie just knew it would slowly get to him the more people asked about it.

Jeanie hoped Shuller was really holding up and not just putting up a front. However, if that was the case, if he was just holding it together, eventually, she knew that the dam would break. She was just hoping it would not be too devastating for him and that she would be able to help when everything bubbled to the surface.

Jeanie was securing a tablecloth to one of the last tables when she happened to glance up. Shuller strode over to her, a genuine smile across his face. Jeanie quickly finished her task and walked to meet him.

"I thought you were going to come later," she said as the met him mid-field.

"Figured the sooner I get here the better." She could tell there was something lurking behind that smile. Was it fear? He knew as she did it was going to be a long trying day. He was grateful that he had Jeanie. The thought of having her alongside him made what the day was to bring more bearable.

"Need any more help?"

"I'm sure the ladies could put you to work," Jeanie said with a sly smile.

"I can imagine. Well, we have what, like, another hour or so before things kick off. Better get a move on." With that, Shuller and Jeanie walked over to check in with Kelly and the rest of the committee members to help set up the craft and food booths before the crowd starts descending upon the park.

Shuller and Jeanie helped set up the remaining tables just as the town slowly started filtering into the park. The weather was warm for a summer day, not the brutal heat the Arizona summer could bring. It was not long before the park was loaded with townspeople. There was soon a park full of people enjoying the activities and, as expected, slowly making their way over to Shuller. What was unexpected was the questions were mostly about him, not so much about the investigation. He had prepared the standard party-line response to the question requesting an investigation status check, but people seemed to know enough not to ask. That was a small relief to both Jeanie and Shuller.

"You've got a real talent here," Shuller said to the vendor behind the table. Jeanie and Shuller had stopped to browse through a table of various beaded trinkets and bobbles. "It must take you hours to create some of these pieces."

"Some, yes," she said proudly. She watched as Jeanie picked up a few jewelry sets and looked them over.

"They are very intricate," Jeanie said. She had been eyeing a few pieces in particular. Shuller, too, took notice.

"You seem to like that set very much," he remarked.

"Yes. It matches a dress I just bought. I think it would go perfectly."

Shuller smiled and nodded over to the vendor regarding the set Jeanie was still holding.

"Ten," the vendor replied.

"Oh you don't have to," Jeanie tried to say, but Shuller was already pulling out his wallet.

PRODIGAL SON

"What? You said it would go perfect with that dress. Now, I just have to find a place to bring you out so you have a reason to wear both."

Jeanie raised her eyebrows in surprise. She could not help the smile that crossed her face. She was really taken with how forward Shuller was being at that moment. He actually referenced their relationship in front of someone. That alone was as special as the gift he had just bought her.

The day was not as harsh as he had originally expected. There were various and frequent mentions, but all were in the spirit of well wishes and fond stories of Vivian. Just prior to the annual softball game, Shuller felt he had to address the crowd.

"I wanted to take a brief moment to say thank you for all your well wishes and fond sentiments of our dear Vivian Nash. Your support during this time has been invaluable. We are avidly working to bring her justice, and I think I can speak on behalf of the boys at the station; your cooperation during this time is greatly appreciated. The Commerce Department has been great by setting up donation stations on behalf of Vivian to help pay for her services. As you know, our dear Vivian was on her own, and I wanted to thank personally all who have donated thus far. On behalf of my boys from the station, and the guys from the firehouse, we would like to contribute our annual wager for our softball game toward the service as well. With that, let's get this game going!"

The crowd cheered as Shuller joined the rest of his team along the sideline for the start of the game.

"Hey Chief, here's to a good game," Shuller crossed over to the chief with his hand extended. The chief gladly accepted his hand and shook it firmly.

"Do me a favor?" Shuller leaned in, "No easy wins here, okay? Just a regular game, okay?"

The chief gave Shuller a curt nod.

"I'll make sure the guys don't hold back. Have a good game," the chief said and returned to his place as second baseman.

The crowd really got into the game, as usual, for the event. The game was a tight battle for supremacy. The score was traded back and forth for most of the game. At the bottom of the ninth, the score was tied, nine-nine. Frank was up to bat. Shuller was on second, Danny on first. Frank had got ahold of that pitch and turned it into a double, which is what Shuller figured he'd need to beat the throw at the plate.

Shuller already saw the center fielder back pedaling as he took off from the bag. Shuller rounded third and chanced a glance toward center field. The firefighter was fumbling backwards as he failed to make the catch. Shuller kicked it into gear and ran toward the plate. Just then, the center fielder recovered enough to make the throw to the cutoff man, but the shortstop did not have time to throw to home. As soon as crossed the plate, the game was over. Shuller trotted to a stop and hunched over, trying to catch his breath.

With the game officially over, the crowd rushed the field to congratulate the players. Jeanie bounded over to Shuller and threw her arms around him. Caught up in the moment, Shuller scooped her up and kissed her there at the plate. It was the first public confirmation of what the town was gossiping about already.

Shuller realized it a moment too late, but then decided not to care and deepened the kiss. The kiss did not go unnoticed by the crowd either. It started a lot of talk amongst the crowd before the kiss had even ended. It became a brief distraction from the other talk that had been circulating around the town the last few days.

KATHLEEN LOPEZ

PRODIGAL SON

Chapter Nine

"The lilies would be very nice," the funeral director said. He scribbled down some selections Shuller made regarding Vivian's funeral. He took on the responsibility of arranging the services for her. He felt that it was his obligation; it was what he had to do for her.

"Is there anything else that needs to be taken care of?"

"Once the body is released from the coroner's office, we can take it from there." The director was trying to be sensitive to both Shuller's feeling toward Vivian and the fact that he didn't want to push upon him that everything hinged on waiting for the police. The investigation turned up little to nothing with regards of evidence or leads. There was no witnesses, no real prints to assist, no motive, nothing. It was so random and isolated that there weren't any hints of a trail.

"Uh, yes. I'll see if we can get you an update on that," Shuller stammered. He knew there was no update. He also knew that they would have to release the body sooner rather than later. While it would not be a complete form of closure, he, as did the town, needed to have a proper funeral for the poor woman.

Shuller was more distracted than he had thought he would be today. Dealing with Vivian's funeral arrangements aside, today he was going to the house. It had been some time since that night and he had yet to step foot in the house. His stomach ached at the very thought of stepping foot in that house, not to mention even attempting to go into her room.

Shuller rose from the wooden chair of the funeral director's office. The director mirrored him and came around his desk to lead the sheriff to the front door.

"My sincere condolences," he offered as they reached the exit.

Shuller felt odd still receiving condolences on behalf of Vivian. He was not family after all, or was he, if only technically? Shuller's only response was a curt nod before he left. The morning sky greeted him as he slowly trudged to his car. The warm breeze, distant bird song, and general serene of the morning seemed to be a juxtaposition to what lay ahead of him. Shuller sighed as he climbed into his car and started out for her house.

He ran over the checklist in his mind. First, he would check around to see if he would notice anything out of place. That alone would be difficult as there had been techs roaming over that house in days past and there were bound to be things out of place. Besides, what did he expect to find that they had not already reviewed? Then there was the task of organizing her belongings. In the days after her death, it was discovered that Vivian was a practical woman. She had filed a will with the law offices on the edge of town. She knew that if there were any family left anywhere, they would not be able to handle her estate in the event of her death. She was one of the younger ones left as it was of what little distant relatives that existed. She had left it all to Shuller. No one had found that odd really. Well no one, but Shuller. He felt strange about having the responsibility, but at the same time, he knew he did not trust anyone else to handle it properly.

This was one of the main reasons he had distanced himself from the investigation. The fact she had left him everything, it did not seem above board that he run the investigation as well. Danny was doing the best he could have possibly expected with this case.

PRODIGAL SON

Shuller was overwhelmed with trying to deal with her death and her property. He could not officially do anything with her things or the house just yet, though. It was still a crime scene.

God, who's going to want to live there now? he wondered as he drove. *No one is going to want to buy it. What the hell am I going to do with it?*

Before he came to any conclusion to that problem, he was turning onto Cedar Mill Lane. As he rounded the corner, his eyes distinctively were drawn to her house. The yellow police tape draped across her porch caught his attention straight off. Shuller parked his car and took yet another steadying breath.

As he started to cross the street, he saw Danny waiting for him at the edge of her walk. Danny offered to meet him to help provide a walk through.

"Boss," Danny acknowledged as Shuller approached.

"Morning, Danny." Shuller's eyes moved from Danny to the house behind him. "Going to be a long morning," he huffed.

Danny simply nodded with a tight-lipped smile and turned to lead the way in. Shuller felt like he was walking through wet sand. His eyes drifted up the exterior of the house. The structure began to loom over him as he passed beneath its shadow.

They stepped around the caution tape crisscrossing the porch. Danny unlocked the door and stepped inside. Shuller took another steadying breath and followed.

Quick, like a ripping off a band aide, he thought, that way he did not have to think too much about where he was going and what he was going to see.

The first floor looked virtually untouched. There was barely a knick-knack out of place, as if Viv had just stepped out. The air was stale, Shuller noted.

Danny gave Shuller a moment to look around, to adjust. He was in uncharted territory and was not sure just what the sheriff was going to do or react to. He found that Shuller was calm, but then he rationalized that it was due to only being on the first floor. What would cause the man to run to therapy awaited them upstairs.

"So, he came in through the backdoor," Shuller started off, "and headed upstairs. Passing up any silverware, or any valuables here. This wasn't just a typical B and E."

"Yeah. Seems there was intent. Who or why, as you know…" Danny trailed off. No one ever said anything but a kind word about Vivian Nash.

Shuller had turned and listened to Danny. His gaze then moved to the stairs behind him. Stairs that he knew led to the bedrooms, or to be clinical, the crime scene. His eyes rolled back slightly as he closed them. A steadying breath was not going to cut it this time. Shuller nodded toward the staircase. Danny glanced over his shoulder and again, simply nodded back, and turned to lead the way up the stairs.

His steps were deliberate and slow, as were Shuller's behind him. Danny knew there was little to be seen, compared to that night, but still, the shock of it to Shuller was the thought running through his mind. While the stains had all run dark and the initial horror of it all was behind Danny, what lay down the hall may have a definite impact for the man following him.

They reached the top of the stairs and Danny stepped aside. He let Shuller determine what to do next. While he was not a part of the investigation, Danny knew that Shuller would not do anything to contaminate what little they had of a crime scene.

Shuller passed Danny and stood in the hallway. Despite being behind him, Danny still found himself averting his eyes from the man. He only looked up when he heard Shuller take his next steps. He noted that they were in the opposite way from Vivian's bedroom.

"So the call was made from here then?" Shuller asked, breaking the silence.

"Uh, yeah. We figured she heard a noise and came down here to the spare room to make a call. Not sure why, though. Perhaps she tried to hide? I mean she has a phone in her room, too."

"It's broken," Shuller said, his voice cracking. "She knocked it over once and something inside was rattling she told me. I kept asking if she wanted me to get her a new one, and she kept putting it off. Said she'd get around to it herself. Guess not," he said with a grimace.

"Ah. Well, that explains that then." Danny remained by the top of the stairs. He figured he would give Shuller enough space to work all this out himself.

Shuller had turned to listen to Danny. That was when his gaze shifted from the man hugging the wall to the room at the end of the hall. There was little to see from his angle, but he did notice a faint pattern that adorned the far wall of her bedroom. A burning feeling built in Shuller's chest. He inhaled sharply as if it hurt to breathe. His eyes followed the pattern until it disappeared from his view, obstructed by the doorframe. Shuller turned and slowly approached the room.

Danny watched Shuller as he crossed in front of him. He was not sure what to do, if anything. He watched as Shuller approached the doorway, hesitated, and then took a step into the room. Danny raised an eyebrow, vacated his post along the wall, and moved behind him.

Shuller's gaze was still trained to the stains along the wall. He continued to follow it down until it reached the bedding. He scanned the length of the bed. His eyes picked up more of the trail of blood up the wall, onto the ceiling. It was as if he avoided the most obvious portion of the room. After examining the surroundings, his eyes finally fell to the floor. The hardwood of the bedroom floor was encrusted with her blood. Shuller felt himself stop breathing. His gaze followed the edge of the dried pool. He noted that it stopped only a few feet from the doorway in which he stood. He noted the outline of where the bat had come to a rest.

Shuller could not hear a sound. All the air was sucked from the room. He barely registered Danny coming up behind him. He had not heard him until he put his hand on his shoulder.

"Boss? You alright?"

"Uh, yeah. Yeah Danny. I'm...damn," Shuller said absentmindedly. It was then he noticed that the blood splatter was not only reserved to the walls, but the ceiling, too. Shuller closed his eyes and shook his head. He bustled past Danny to get out of the room. He felt as if he was going to pass out. He did not stop until he reached the banister of the staircase. He took a tight grip of the handrail and stared down the staircase to the first floor landing. Danny eased out of the room and into the hallway.

"Sorry, boss." Danny was at a loss as for what to say.

"No worries, Danny. It's just…it's alright." Shuller slowly righted himself as he released his grip on the banister. It was then he noticed the faint scuff marks along the floor.

"Bastard couldn't even leave us a shoe print, huh?"

"Yeah. He knew what he was doing, or he's seen too much NCIS or something."

"I see what you mean on not getting much from the room. Still no freaking idea as to why though." Shuller was not asking Danny as much as venting his frustrations.

"If the bastard came in from the back, then his shoes would have been dirty or muddy. The idea is he came in from the void, right?"

"Yeah, but it's too marshy for any prints, and if he did, by the time he walked across her backyard, any mud would have been wiped off his shoes."

Shuller rubbed his head in aggravation.

"I hate to say this, but thank goodness she had no family left. God, could you imagine if we had a gaggle of angry family members wanting to know what happened? What the hell would we tell them?"

"Sad, but true boss."

Shuller sighed. He put his hands on his waist and stood for a moment. "Venture it is safe enough for me to go upstairs?"

"Upstairs?"

"Yeah. There's a staircase behind that door there," he pointed to the door across from the spare room. "Viv pretty much closed off the top floor years ago after her husband died. She said she used it mostly for storage. Dunno. Never been up there myself. Thought maybe I could start sifting through the stuff to see if there are any skeletons in the closet that will make sense of this. Not sure what I'll find."

"Actually, we never considered going upstairs. All the action seemed to be focused right here," Danny said motioning around the hallway. "I guess as long as…"

"I've got gloves, Danny. If anything jumps out as odd, I'll give you a holler."

Danny nodded as Shuller made his way passed the spare room, opened the door, revealing the base of the staircase leading to the third floor. The steps creaked as he trotted up. He pulled the white latex gloves from his back pocket and had put them on by the time he reached the top. He felt along the wall for a light switch.

Vivian wasn't kidding about closing this all off, he thought to himself. The air was thick and musky.

A dark curtain blocked any light from the window that was at the end of the hall; unlike its twin on the second floor where the sunlight flooded the hallway with an array of colors from the stained glass. While the house didn't have an attic space, this third floor had more than made up for that. There was no furniture in the rooms. They were repurposed long ago to hold boxes and various odd memorabilia she and her husband had collected long ago.

Shuller crossed over to the window and pulled back the heavy drapery. He was rewarded by a dust cloud that practically choked the air from him. He noticed once the hallway was better illuminated, the floor had a fine sheen of dust as well. His were also the only footprints.

Danny was right; all the action was on the second floor. Looks like no one has been up here in years.

Despite being the only person up there in who knows how long, he decided to keep his gloves on. It was a matter of cleanliness rather than preservation of evidence now. The third floor was meant to be more for living than storage. Vivian being on her own after her husband passed, there was no need for her to venture onto yet another empty floor, so she converted it to more of an easy access attic.

Each room seemed to contain various boxes and trunks. Shuller pondered what she could have been storing and why. Who was all this for in the end? What would she need to store things that she apparently had no need to access?

Shuller entered the first room to his left. It had appeared its original purpose was to be a bedroom. The room had random boxes and some curious items, such as a dress form manikin in the back corner.

"Guess she used to sew," Shuller said. He moved into the room and eyed a few boxes. Thankfully, they were all clearly labeled. Shuller was relieved that he did not have to sift through all the boxes, assuming they were all labelled correctly. Vivian was meticulous so he did not feel the need to second-guess each box's description. Most were labeled "Tax Records," "Insurance" and such. They were the typical and mundane items to keep. He ran his gaze over the various banker boxes and did not see anything that required him to sort so he moved onto the next room.

The second bedroom passed the unused bathroom was in a similar state. More banker boxes were stacked along the walls; however, this room had a large trunk in the middle of the floor. It begged for attention. Shuller walked over to the window, and learning his lesson from the hallway window, slowly moved aside the heavy drapery. The darkened room flooded with light. Shuller looked out the back window for a moment. He was able to see the immediate neighbor's backyards as well as those across the void. Everyone either was at work or had recently returned to school. The neighborhood was quiet.

He broke his stare and turned to look at the trunk. It seemed odd to him to have this trunk here when everything else was neatly packed away in banker boxes. He walked back to the trunk and knelt in front of it. Luckily, it was not locked. The heavy lid creaked open as Shuller lifted it and placed it to rest along the boxes that were piled behind it. What he saw in the trunk confused him.

The first thing Shuller saw was baby shoes. Little crocheted blue and white baby shoes.

Viv didn't have any kids, he thought. *Why would she have those?*

Shuller lifted the shoes and looked at them as if they were going to provide a clue spontaneously as to why they were there. Shuller placed them down gently on the floor besides him and was more curious than ever to continue to search the trunk. Beneath where the shoes laid was a manila folder. Shuller picked up the folder and read the tab along the side: "V. Nash, Baby Boy". Shuller felt the wind knocked out of him and sat squarely on the floor.

"They had a kid," he exclaimed without realizing he had so loudly.

"Who did, boss?"

Shuller damn near jumped out of his skin. "Christ, Danny. You should wear a bell or something."

"Sorry, boss. I just came up to check on you. Who are you talking about? Who had a kid?"

"Come here; check this out." Shuller rose to meet Danny as he entered the room. Once by his side, Shuller flipped open the file folder to see hospital paperwork. The papers were old and faded, but the men could read that indeed Vivian had a child, male, in the late seventies, before they moved to the town.

"He'd be in his late thirties now?" Danny questioned. Shuller nodded in agreement.

"Huh. No name is given. What's the deal with that?" Shuller said as he continued to flip through the paperwork in the file.

"Ah, here we go," he said as he flipped through the file. "Seems like the baby was given up shortly after he was born. I can't make out the name of the agency that took him though. There has to be more files in here. Look at all the folders in this box."

"Hmm. Looks like we'll have some digging to do then."

Shuller just stared at Danny not getting the full gist of what he was saying.

"Well, if she did have a child, and he's out there somewhere, this is all his, ain't it?" Danny ventured.

"Yep. You have a point there. Guess I dodged a bullet and won't have to deal with this all myself," Shuller sighed.

"I wouldn't get so hopeful just yet, boss. We are assuming this guy knows he was adopted. Hell, it would be quite a shock to the system to find out at late in life you were adopted. Only to find out your birth mom just died. He may not want to even deal with all of this either. We will need to tread lightly until we know exactly what the situation is here."

"Agreed. Wonder why they gave him up though. She always said she was alone, but apparently not. Why give away your kid? They were always fine. I mean, they had her family money."

"Who knows, boss. They apparently didn't want kids. Some people are like that, I suppose."

"Guess you're right. Well, looks like there are a few more items in the trunk here to go through. Perhaps there is something Suzy Q and I can find to help us sort all this out. Mind giving me a hand? I think we can just gather up some paperwork without having to take the trunk down three flights of stairs."

Danny and Shuller surveyed the random items that were in the trunk. They gathered several folders and a box along with the baby shoes. Shuller wondered mostly about those. If someone was going to give away a child, why buy him or her shoes and keep them?

Danny and Shuller carried the newly found items to Shuller's car.

"I'll head back to the station and start going through this with Suzy Q and see what we can turn up," Shuller said as he dropped all the files onto the passenger seat. He peeled off his gloves and laid them on top of the pile.

"Okay, boss. I'll go ahead and lock up here and see you at the station later."

PRODIGAL SON

Shuller nodded and climbed into his car. The revelation that Viv had a child and never told anyone was still working its way through his brain. It was her prerogative for certain, but she always seemed so lonely at the end, as if she could have used family around her. He wondered if she had come to regret it. Shuller wondered if it was her decision in the end after all. Did she feel she had to give up the child? It had not struck him until then that he hadn't seen her husband's name on the file folder or on what little the paperwork he had seen.

Did Richard even know?

Shuller was complicating the situation more and more in his mind as he drove to the station seemingly on autopilot. He got to the station within minutes and parked in the first spot he saw. He meandered over to the passenger side while he was entertaining all the different reasons and rationales in his head. He scooped up all the items and closed up the car. Shuller entered the station with the box and files and navigated towards Susan's desk. The barely balancing files had just missed making it to her desk as they cascaded to the floor.

"What's all this?" she asked as she help gather the scattered pile of folders.

"We have a little investigating to do. I'm going to need your help with this, and your discretion. Help me with these, would you? We'll set up in my office."

Shuller restacked all the folders on top of the box, placing the crochet booties on top, and headed to his office. Susan followed quickly.

"All this came from Vivian's?" she asked as she closed his office door behind her. She tried to understand what he was holding. She joined him on his couch.

"Okay, spill."

"Well, the third floor of Viv's was basically used for storage. I was going through all of rooms to see what was there since she apparently left it all to me in that makeshift will she had filed with the clerk of courts. In one of the rooms was this trunk where I found all of this." Shuller motioned to the stash he just placed besides the couch.

"I'm still not sure what I am looking at here."

"This was the first thing I came across in the trunk," Shuller said as he held up the booties followed by the folder full of random paperwork.

Susan took the folder while looking quizzically at the dangling booties. She flipped open the folder and started devouring the information she saw. Shuller realized she found her answer as soon as he saw her eyes grow wide. She snapped her head toward Shuller.

"She had a boy? Did you know?"

"Nope. Looks like no one knew. Danny and I were thinking we have to find this guy and let him know what happened. Technically, all of Viv's belongings would go to him."

"Not necessarily," Susan said shaking her head. "If she wanted it to go to him, she would have left it to him in her will. She would have left you some information about him to find him in the event you ever had to. No. I don't think she wanted him to have it."

Shuller was taken aback slightly. "I have to find him, though."

"And what if he doesn't know about any of this, huh?"

"That's what we have to determine. We need to locate him and see if we should approach him."

"She willed everything to you for a reason, Martin." Susan rarely used his first name in the office. When she did, especially with a tone in her voice, Shuller realized she was trying to get him to realize the full impact of a situation.

"I know. But since it is mine to deal with, I choose to deal with it this way. We will take care in the situation. I'm not going to barge into this guy's life like a bull in a china shop. We'll assess as we go. Deal?"

"Proceed with caution, yes," Susan relented.

"Besides, don't you want to know?" He teased her. "I mean, here is yet another loose end in all of this. I hate loose ends."

"Life is made up of a lot of loose ends sometimes," she murmured.

"Well, that's a case killer. We need some answers in this one. I'll take anything right now."

"Since when is this a case?" Susan asked, looking at the stack of folders.

"Nothing makes sense here. Her murder, a kid no one knew about. I need answers somewhere for something. This all is just driving me mad."

Shuller took back his folder to review while Susan grabbed another for herself to start sorting through. They sat on the couch in silence as they flipped page after page. After a few pages, Shuller popped up and grabbed two notepads from his drawer and a couple of pens. He handed one of each to Susan before he set down and started scribbling some notes on his pad. Before too long, Susan was doing the same. They spent a majority of the afternoon thumbing through papers and jotting down notes.

Shuller had finished his folder while Susan was making a last notation on her pad.

"Alright. Let's see what we got here. What I have is that in 1977, Vivian gave birth to a baby boy," Susan pointed out. "From there it seems she found a group home, or what we could call an orphanage, for the child as it looks like they had taken him in as an infant. I have a few reports from the agency, a letter or two about his progress, and just general information. There's not too much in this folder. It looks like she has a lot of info on him if she had this many file folders for him. For someone who gave up her kid, she still kept track of him. I guess she tracked him until she knew he was taken care of. Doesn't sound like she wanted to give him up. I wonder why she did. I think I'm missing some paperwork here. I'll keep digging, but that's all I have so far."

"There is something missing. I noticed it before," Shuller started.

"Something missing?"

"Did you happen to notice all the paperwork so far is only in her name? Not one mention of Richard anywhere." Shuller cocked his head toward Susan.

"What are you getting at?"

"I'm just saying, maybe Richard didn't know. They were married before 1977. Maybe he didn't want children, and when she got pregnant, she gave the kid up."

"How was he not going to notice his wife was pregnant?" Susan questioned.

"I don't know. Maybe they were separated?"

"Let's see what we can find out there. Where were Vivian and Richard in 1977? If they were separated, then that would explain how she could be pregnant and he'd not known."

Shuller did not know those type of intimate details, apparently, of her life to answer Susan.

Susan gave Shuller a head nod and leapt off the couch. "Mind if I use your computer?"

"Actually, I would prefer it."

Susan started typing away looking for residential records. Then Susan had an epiphany. A few click and frantic tapping of the keyboard and she had her answer.

"The military," she said triumphantly. "Richard was in the military," she said triumphantly. "Give me a few minutes here and, yes, he stationed overseas for what looks like a whole year or so. Ha! Oh."

"Oh?"

"Well, it would appear he was gone that whole year. Um...oh come on, really? Do I have to explain the birds and the bees to you? If he was gone the whole year..."

"Then it probably wasn't his kid."

"Yep. That's why his name was not on any of the paperwork. Vivian had an affair while he was away, got pregnant, and gave up the kid. Oh, wow," Susan said.

"It would explain why she kept track of a kid that she gave away. She didn't want to give him away, but felt she had to. Oh, brother. This just got ugly."

"How do you feel about finding him now, huh? Not only do you have to find him and hope he knows he's adopted, but now have to tell him he was product of some one-night-stand or something and was given away to hide evidence."

"That's cold, Suz."

"I only report what I see, Sheriff."

"Well, we can always determine if he knows and ..."

"If you are suggesting we let him find it and figure it out for himself, I'm coming over there and slapping you."

"I don't know. This all just got messy. Ugh. I guess the next step is for you to start digging more into these folders. Maybe there is more info here that will lead somewhere," he suggested.

"Okay. I'm on it. I'll dig through all the other paperwork you got here, but it's getting late. Don't you have plans tonight?"

"Huh? Oh yeah, dinner. Wait," he turned to Susan with a confused look on his face.

PRODIGAL SON

"We're best friends, you dolt. Now get. You can't, or rather, you better not take her out looking like that." Susan smiled and continued tapping away at the keyboard.

Shuller just smirked and left his office without further antagonizing her. He was able to duck out of the office without being stopped by anyone. A small miracle on most days. He headed straight for his car and took off for home. He was looking forward to unwinding with Jeanie. They decided to have just a night out for dinner. There was nothing good out in the theaters, so dinner, and then most likely back to her place. Shuller's townhouse down by the movie theater was nice enough, if you enjoy sparse living. He was never one for decorating or entertaining. It was a place to hang his hat.

Shuller made it home and parked in the driveway. He bounded up the stairs to the front door. He attributed the second wind to getting to see her again tonight. He entered the house and quickly headed to the master bathroom. He had not realized the time and only had about an hour and a half before he had to meet Jeanie.

A quick shower, ooh, and a quick shave should do it, he thought as he caught his reflection in the mirror.

He turned on the shower then headed to the closet for a suitable outfit. His wardrobe was as sparse as his decor. Besides his work uniforms, Shuller owned very little outside of a few slacks, jeans and a variety of shirts. He selected a dark pair of slacks and a maroon button down shirt.

He shrugged off his work clothes into a heap outside the shower and stepped into the strong stream of warm water. Usually he would take his time and wash away the day of drama he had at the office, but it was a quick scrub up and get out. He did find himself, all though briefly, flashing back to today's discovery. Vivian had a son out there. He thought of her all alone in that house, needlessly. Shuller wondered why she did not tell Richard, although he suspected why she hadn't. Suzy Q's assessment may have been closest to the pin.

Enough, he thought. Shuller shook his head and rinsed the soap from his hair and body before shutting off the taps. He stepped out of the shower and was greeted with a blast of cold air. He quickly wrapped a towel around his waist. Apparently, his daydreaming took a bit more than a few moments. The bathroom was hazy with steam and the mirror was completely frosted over.

Shuller made haste as he dried himself off and then rubbed his head with the towel. His hair was getting long by his standards. It was practically touching his ears and collar. He made a mental note to get a haircut this time. Shuller proceeded to get dressed and ready to meet Jeanie.

Shirt, slacks, socks, shoes, wallet, phone, and keys and out the door. After locking up, he bounded down the steps as quickly as he had when he arrived home. Shuller realized he was humming a tune, but once the realization hit him, he could not recall the name of the song. He climbed into his car and started her up.

A stoplight or two to Jeanie's house was all that was standing in his way. He turned up the radio a bit but did not pay much mind to what was playing. That did not stop him from drumming along on the steering wheel at the last light on his journey. At the light, he peered to the left and caught sight of her house. The smile grew on his face without a thought. The light changed and he made the left, never once looking to the right like he had so many times before toward Viv's house.

PRODIGAL SON

He found a spot right in front of her house and parked. Shuller took one of his steadying breaths. He realized his heart was racing a bit.

Nerves? Nah, he thought, just excitement.

Shuller had not realized just when, nor had he stopped to think about the fact that he was in a full on relationship. He and Jeanie had been seeing each other for a little while now. It was safe to call them officially "a thing." Shuller chuckled to himself at the thought.

"Well, can't get you to the restaurant from here, can I?" he said aloud as he finally got out of the car. He tried consciously to slow his pace to her front door. He did not want to seem as anxious as he truly felt. He reached her front door and rang the bell.

Jeanie was in the kitchen putting away the last dish from the dishwasher. She had busied herself while she waited for Shuller to arrive. She smiled when she heard the bell and made her way to the front door.

"Well, don't you look handsome," she said, leaning on the opened door. Shuller returned the smile she was beaming at him.

"Just trying to keep up with my company," he replied. "About ready?"

"Two secs. Come in while I get my bag?"

Shuller nodded and smiled. Jeanie left the hallway to grab her things from the kitchen table. Shuller simply loitered just inside the doorway while he waited for her. It was not a long wait as she was soon walking toward him. Just as Jeanie came within arm's reach, he slipped an arm around her waist and pulled her toward him.

Something about the way she was smiling, Shuller found he could not help himself. Jeanie, though a bit startled, gave him no resistance.

While one arm encircled her, the other had found purchase on her cheek. He slowly pulled her closer to him. His lips gently brushed hers, as if seeking permission. Jeanie gasped slightly before sighing and melting to his touch. That was the only sign he needed, and Shuller then captured her lips with his own. It was a simple and gentle kiss. His grip tightened around her as she held onto his arms for support. The brief kiss concluded with Shuller simply pulling back slightly, without releasing her from his hold.

"Sorry. Couldn't resist," he said, a smile spreading slowly across his face. Jeanie had rested her forehead to his.

"No complaints from me." Jeanie regained her composure and then proceeded to wipe her lipstick from his lips.

"While I hate to break this up, our reservation is in thirty minutes."

"Mmm. Yeah. Yeah," Shuller replied, breaking his own trance. He was still smiling as he slowly released Jeanie and stretched out his hand toward the still open door. Jeanie smiled back and passed in front of him, waited for Shuller to follow, then locked up. Shuller presented his arm for Jeanie as he escorted her to the car.

The ride to the restaurant consisted of idle chitchat and plenty of smiles exchanged. They were headed to the new restaurant just outside of town. It was a bit dressier than the town's diner was, and Shuller enjoyed the change. By Jeanie's appearance, so did she.

They sat at a table off to the side by the fireplace. It was too warm for a fire, but the look was still romantic. Jeanie and Shuller were looking over the menu when they heard the buzzing.

"Is that yours?" Jeanie asked. Shuller dug in his pocket for his cell phone. It was a text from Susan. "Are they calling you in?"

Shuller detected a slight bit of disappointment in her tone.

"No. Suzy Q was just texting me something about a case." Shuller looked at the message and felt his own pang of disappointment.

More questions than answers in the other folders. Trying to piece it all together, but need to keep digging.

"I take it it's not what you wanted to read?"

"Uh, no. Just hit another dead end." Shuller texted her back to quit working for the day and they would look at options tomorrow.

"Anything to do with Viv? Or can you not tell me?"

"Actually, yes and no. Well, Danny and I came across something today at her house and Suzy Q and I were trying to track it down. Looks like it didn't pan out."

"Oh, do you guys have a suspect?"

"No." He barely contained his own disappointment. "It looks like we may have unearthed a relative," Shuller hushed his tone and leaned across the table slightly. Jeanie followed suit. "It would seem Viv had a son. We found birth records and orphanage paperwork. Suzy was just texting to tell me that she not having much luck with all the information we found at Viv's. I just want to know how to find the guy."

"Whoa, she had a kid? They never said anything about ever having children," Jeanie said quietly.

"Well, that's the thing. Looks like she gave him up while Richard was in the service. Very weird." Shuller made a face. He felt bad talking about Vivian like this, but it was sensational, especially for her.

Both had leaned back in their seats as the waitress came around for their order. With the order placed, Jeanie waited until they were a safe distance before she spoke again.

"So what are you going to do now?"

"Well I feel we need to find this guy. Suzy's concerned if the guy doesn't know about her, but I think he has a right to know and the option if he wants to deal with her estate and all. If not, I'll go back to dealing with all of it. I was just hoping to find him right off. Crazy I know, but, I mean, the funeral is tomorrow after all."

It was the first time since that morning that he had thought about it. Just this morning, he was picking out the flowers. Suddenly, the impact of the funeral being so soon hit him.

"Well, she'll finally be put to rest, the poor dear. Tomorrow will be a bit hard, but you'll have me," Jeanie said with a smile and a cock of the head. Shuller returned a smile, however weak.

"So, have you spoken to your family lately?" Jeanie took the opportunity to ask more of his family. "I know you said you guys weren't so close any more, but when you're dealing with all of this, sometimes it makes you want to reconnect."

"Not really," he sighed. "We haven't kept in touch much over the years. I last spoke to my kid sister about a month or so ago. She emailed me pics of the kids. Her youngest is about to graduate elementary school soon. She suggested I come out to New York, meet up either at her place upstate or out by my brother. I don't see myself fitting into Manhattan."

"No, but it would be a nice place to visit though."

"What's with all the family talk, anyway?"

"Well, you seem upset about Vivian not having family around, when it seems like she apparently gave hers away. I just didn't want you to give up on yours."

"That's sweet, but we still talk. Not every day, but we touch base more often than not. But I see your point. Perhaps we can head out there for a few days, like in the fall or something, before the snow."

"We?" Jeanie smiled wide.

Shuller shook his head and chuckled. The waitress appeared with their food. The conversation then drifted to more common day topics and dwelled less on the sensational.

Shuller jumped at the sound of the alarm clock. He scrambled to stop the screeching as quickly as he could. The blaring numbers of 8:30 stared back at him unforgivingly. He lay back for a moment. His thoughts went straight back to last night. He sighed heavily, wishing he had only stayed over Jeanie's last night. It was getting to the point where someone was going to have a drawer of clothes at the others eventually, and again, his place had a lot to be desired. His thoughts were quickly replaced by the dawning realization of the events of the day. Vivian's funeral. Shuller pulled himself up and swung his feet over the side of the bed. He glanced up at the suit that hung off the back of the closet door. He had it dry cleaned and pressed for the day.

He got up for what was going to be a long day. Getting ready to go out this time was certainly not as enjoyable as the previous evening's preparations. He got dressed and ready rather quickly despite feeling as he was trudging through quick sand. In no time, he was already on his way to pick up Jeanie. Despite seeing her again so quickly after last night, he was not as excited given their ultimate destination.

The whole town seemed to crowd into the cemetery for the service. Shuller decided on a graveside service. Vivian was not much of a churchgoer he noted. By the time Shuller and Jeanie arrived, there was barely a spot left to park. Shuller was glad to see that the notice in the local paper brought everyone out for her. He felt it was a proper send off.

The service was brief; again, Shuller thought she would appreciate that as well. Despite its brevity, Shuller found himself scanning the crowd. He was not sure if it was just out of awe that everyone showed up, or if he was stuck in cop mode. He felt as if he was looking for something, or someone. After all, it was a possibility that the killer came to the funeral.

Shuller looked at all the saddened faces of the town folk that showed up to pay their respects. The murmur of the clergyman droned on in the background. Then, he saw something that stood out just a bit to him. His gaze fell on a man who was standing just off the edge of the pack. He stood out a bit not only for the fact that he was physically removed from the crowd, but he didn't have the same sorrowful expression. He was not crying, not frowning, not anything. He was just there. Staring straight ahead. He seemed unmoved. Jeanie squeezed his arm and snapped him back to the current situation. He gave a tight-lipped smile to her look of concern. Shuller made a mental note that something seemed off about that guy, something he didn't like at all.

After the service, people gathered up in small groups and chattered on about various antidotes about Vivian. Shuller excused himself from Jeanie and made his way through the crowd toward Levi. He just wanted to shake the vibe he felt about this guy. Levi was already making his way to his 'Stang when Shuller called out to him.

"Hey!" Shuller yelled as he jogged over to Levi.

"Huh?" Levi uttered as he turned to face a trotting Shuller.

"I just wanted to thank you for coming. You're the new mechanic, right? Over on Emerson? The shop works on the squad cars for us on occasion."

"Yeah. Levi," he said plainly.

"Levi, oh like the jeans?"

Levi sighed heavily and barely contained an eye roll.

"Yes, like the jeans," he huffed out with a deadpan expression. Shuller took that to mean the poor bastard had gotten that most of his life.

"Well, I just wanted to thank you for coming today. I didn't realize you knew her."

"Nope, didn't know her, but figured the town was coming out, so I probably should to. If you'll excuse me, I have to head back to the shop."

"Ah, yes, sure. Thanks again." With that, Levi gave a quick nod of the head and continued onto his car.

Shuller didn't like this guy. He just could not put a finger on it yet as to why.

PRODIGAL SON

Chapter Ten

With the service finally over and behind him, Shuller's was able to shift his attention once more to the potential heir of the Nash estate. He tried not to feel slighted or hurt Vivian never confided in him that she once had a son. He had rationalized that away after all. They were just friends really. Why would he have expected her to confide all of her life's secrets to him?

He was just some guy that checked in on her, looked after her, he thought. So much so, in fact, that she left him her estate. No, why would that warrant telling of a massive secret?

Danny knocked on the open office door. "Boss? You wanted to see me?"

"Come in, Danny. I was wondering if you and the boys had finished talking to everyone on your short list regarding Viv's case."

"Short list? What short list?" he absentmindedly snorted. "We spoke to neighbors and such, but there was not, hasn't been a short list of anyone for this case. You've seen the file. There's not much to go on."

"So no short list. Great," Shuller huffed. He tapped his pen on his desk absentmindedly.

"Well, let's start making one then. I'd like you to go to the garage down off Emerson. Talk to the head mechanic there."

"You want me to go and talk to the head mechanic at the auto shop? Is there any reason why I would be doing that, boss?" Danny asked, confused by the request.

KATHLEEN LOPEZ

"Yeah. He's now on the short list of people to start interviewing again."

Danny merely shrugged at his boss in passive acceptance at his request, despite his confusion.

"Oh, and do yourself a favor and save yourself some grief. Don't mention the jeans."

"Jeans? Why? What the heck's wrong with this guy's jeans?" Danny wondered.

"Not his … just trust me. It will hit you later."

"O-Okay," Danny said questionably. He was about to leave when he figured he would try to gain some understanding to his latest assignment. "By the way, why him? What gets this guy on the short list? Well, the only guy on the short-list anyway? I mean, it seems kind of random to me," Danny asked, puzzled.

"I saw him at the service yesterday. He seemed to stick out like a sore thumb. It just looked weird to me. Dunno. It could be nothing, but it just struck me as odd that he was there."

"Uh, boss, everyone was there," Danny seemingly tried to justify.

"Yeah, I know. Call it a hunch or whatever. I remembered in the file it saying he didn't know her. Why was he there, really?"

"The town practically shut down to go out to send her off, boss," Danny offered. "We all did. Just cause this guy hasn't lived in town all his life and knew her like you, doesn't call into suspect why he paid respects to her."

"I don't know. It's like an arsonist. They set fire to a building, but then come back and watch the firemen come to put it out. Who knows why wackos do the things they do? It struck me

188

odd that he was there despite the whole town being there. He didn't seem like he was there to pay respects. He was just there, watching. It gave me the creeps to be honest. I already have Suzie Q looking up his background for me. Just go and question him, would you?"

"What should I be asking him? Usually 'short list' people have a reason they're on the short list. A creepy funeral goer isn't much to go on."

Shuller shot him a look before offering a line of questioning. "Just say you're doing follow up on those we already spoke to before. See if you can get a read on him. Try to dig up what you can about him without tipping our hand," Shuller said as he leaned back in his chair.

"I have a hand to tip?" Danny asked, semi-annoyed at the seemingly useless task.

"Look, just go talk to the guy. See if you see what I'm talking about at least. There is something about him being there that seemed all wrong to me."

"You got it, boss. I'll head out now in fact." Danny left Shuller's office still a bit sideways on what exactly he would be asking this guy. He swung by his desk for a pad, pen, and his keys. He headed straight out of the police parking lot to the garage. The whole time he wondered what the heck he was going to ask this guy. There was not much time to think about a solid line of questioning during the ride since the auto shop was only a few minutes from the station.

Hell, I should have walked. At least it would have given me more time to figure out what the hell I'm doing, he thought. He was not sure about Shuller's angle with this guy. He had just made up then added him to a short list of suspects without anything more that the justification of "he gave him the creeps."

Danny tried to come up with an approach as he turned onto Emerson. He parked off to the side of the garage so the car would be out of the way. It was only a short walk around to the garage bays from there. As he approached the garage, Danny caught the attention of a guy changing the brakes on someone's Ford. The red and white embroidered patch on his coveralls read "Mike".

"Mike? Hey, I'm looking for the head mechanic here. Any chance he's around?"

"Yeah, he's over by the tires, in bay one." He motioned with the wrench in his hand before he continued his work.

Danny thanked him and crossed over the two bays to get to the tire station. There he stood in his grease smeared blue coveralls. His embroidered tag read "Levi".

Do yourself a favor...trust me it will hit you later, echoed in his head. *Ah!*

Levi saw Danny approaching him. He stood, half anticipating the annoying comparison of his name. He had come to expect it whenever he met someone new. Danny was certainly someone new, at least to him. Thankfully for both of them, though, the comparison it didn't come.

"Hi, Levi. I'm Danny Reynolds with the sheriff department. Do you have a few minutes to answer a couple of questions?"

"Sure." Levi didn't seem too put out to stop working for a bit.

Danny noted that he also certainly didn't seem put out that a sheriff's deputy came over to ask a few questions. He half expected at least a question as to why or a strange facial expression.

"You were at the funeral for Vivian Nash yesterday."

"Was that a question?"

Danny's eyebrows shot up as he noted the irritated tone right off. This guy was going to be a real pain in the ass he thought, but then continued. "Well, according to the report filed from another officer involved in her case, when you were questioned initially about Ms. Nash, you noted that you didn't really know her. I'm curious, if you didn't know her, then why were you there at her funeral?"

"Everyone in town was there. Wouldn't it look odd if I wasn't?"

That was the same point he brought up to Shuller before this little venture. Danny figured he'd poke the bear a bit and see if he got the same vibe as Shuller.

"Why would you care if it looked odd?" Danny didn't mind pushing a few buttons, not since Levi opened the door to being a jerk from the get go. He just wanted to see where this went. It was a valid point. Why not be where the whole town was after all? Then again, since he was there really as a temperature check on this guy, why not nudge him a bit to see what broke loose.

"Like I said, you didn't know her. Funerals are not really a fun place to hang out at. Why go to one for someone you didn't know?"

"True, but like *I* said, everyone was going to be there. I didn't think it a big deal to stand there. Heck, the garage owner called to say to close up shop so we could all go and pay our respects. What was I to do? Head home and catch a game on TV? I don't see the big deal of me going to her funeral." Levi was doing little to hide his irritation. He figured he'd try to get that in check before he piqued too much interest.

"She seemed like a nice lady, according to everyone else around here. I didn't see the harm in going. The whole community was out to pay their respects. It seemed like I should have been there, too, given that reason alone." Levi felt his stomach churn with that statement. *Respect. Ha!* He only hoped his true feelings for her didn't show on his face

"Have you had any problems with anyone in town?" Danny figured he'd change it up. See what, if anything, he could get from the guy.

"Why would you ask that?" *Just what was he getting at,* Levi wondered. The sudden jump in questioning threw him.

Danny instantly found his response a bit defensive. *Apparently, I struck a nerve. What was this guy's deal?* "Well, you're relatively new here. Sometimes you don't mesh right away with someone, you know, until you're settled in," Danny replied. He stood trying to interpret Levi's body language. He could not have missed the fact that Levi's posture was rigid.

"Nope. Meshed just fine," Levi said, wiping his hands on an old rag. Levi tried not to project the anger that was slowly simmering beneath the surface. He suddenly became very conscious of his mouth. He didn't want to appear to smirk or grimace at the officer. He felt his left eye twitch slightly. *Breathe.*

"Never had an issue with anyone here," Levi continued, shifting his weight. He certainly didn't hide the look of confusion on his face. It seemed like a strange jump to make, Levi thought.

Danny was starting to understand why Shuller didn't like him. He found himself not liking him either. And, like Shuller, he was not exactly sure why. There was just something he could not put his finger on, but he started to see what Shuller was talking about.

Danny figured he'd push his luck just a bit more to see what he could find out about him.

"Where did you live before you moved out here?" Danny threw another oddball question at him.

Levi shot him a quizzical look. He certainly didn't like the way the questioning was going. It was no longer asking about some woman's death. He quickly realized he was being investigated.

"What does any of this have to do with anything you're investigating? Why are you asking all this about me?"

"Just curious is all. You're new to town, well, relatively new. Just wondering where you lived before now."

"That's all, huh?" Levi huffed. He was not buying it. "Look, is there is a point to all the questions? I'd just really like to get to the point. I don't think it would look good for the boss to see me questioned by the police while there is some murder investigation going on."

"We don't have much information about you, again, since you're relatively new to town. Just getting some background for the file." Danny could see this interview was winding down quickly.

"You need information. On me. For a file on a murder investigation. You don't think I should question why? You have background information on everyone in town for *the file?*"

"Well everyone else has lived here for years. We know them."

"And I'm some stranger that moves to town and what, I'm suspect number one?" Levi felt his face grow hot. Knowing what he knew, he should not push too hard or it would certainly gather a lot of unwanted attention. But he figured he had the justifiable right to be just this side of outraged given the circumstances. Overall, he was just some guy who happened to move to town, for all the police knew.

Danny realized he was not going to get anything further from Levi. After all, he really had nothing on this guy to probe him for answers. He barely had a thread to follow for questions to begin with, truth be told. He was just following up on his boss's hunch.

"I didn't mean to upset you. It's just that we're doing some follow ups is all. You were questioned the morning after her death, and we're just touching base with everyone to see if anything further could be noted for the investigation."

"Nope, not a thing comes to mind." Levi was skeptical, but decided to believe the officer, if only just to get him to stop questioning him about his past "Not sure what I could have heard really being, what, like a block away. Those on either side of her probably would have heard a lot more than I ever could, I would assume." Levi tried to steady his breath. He obviously gave the impression of being bothered; he just was not sure if that helped or harmed him in the long run.

"True. Well, if you remember anything, or hear of anything, please let us know." Danny gave him a tight-lipped smile and a quick nod of the head before turning on his heel to leave the garage bay.

"That went nowhere fast," he muttered to himself as he headed back to his car. "Not sure what boss man was hoping I'd get out of that guy," Danny said as he sat behind the wheel and started up the car. He glanced over at the shop and caught sight of Levi watching him before returning to work.

"There's definitely something not right about that guy." *Guess I should call in to give him a heads up*, he thought as he reached for his phone.

"Hey, Danny," Shuller replied after barely a ring.

Damned caller ID. "Yeah, boss. I'm just leaving the garage. Got nothing out of that guy, but man, do I get where you're coming from. There's something I can't put my finger on."

"I didn't think you'd get a confession out of him, but was hoping for something. At least it's not just me then. There's just something off about that guy. Well, thanks for the trip. See you back at the station." Shuller hung up the phone.

"Take it your errand of having Danny shake down Levi turned up nothing?" Susan retorted.

"Always a ray of sunshine in a dark world, Suz. And no, nothing came of his little talk. At least Danny validated that he gives off a not-so warm and fuzzy vibe."

"Well, same could be said for me most days…don't you dare," Susan cut Shuller off before he got another word out.

Shuller threw his hands up in surrender.

"Anyway, I turned up nothing on Levi's background," she said as she thumbed through her notepad. "Let's see. He was in the state system, a state run children's home. He was in and out of foster homes until the age of nine when he was finally adopted by the Swansons. They were a well-to-do kind of family. From then on, he had what you would call a normal life. Mr. and Mrs. Swanson were killed in a car accident New Year's night by some drunken kid. Levi then dropped out of college, got a job, blah blah blah," Susan finished her summary with shrug and a huff.

Shuller sat and shook his head. *What are we missing here*, he wondered. Susan plopped the notepad she was reading from on Shuller's desk.

"I'm at a loss. We have no point of origin for this guy, no one to question as far as family." Shuller was growing frustrated.

Family. That word struck a chord with Shuller. He scrunched his eyebrows together at the thought that started wiggling through his brain. He leaned back in his chair as he often did. His elbows found the arm rests as he sat back and the fingers on his right hand seemed to be playing an invisible trumpet.

"Okay, what is it?" Susan questioned. "You have that look."

"What look?" Shuller feigned innocence.

"*The* look. You got the whole thing going now, the face, the air horn thing you do when you're working on something. The look you get when you are trying to figure out 'how do I pull this off'. What are you thinking? It looks like a whopper."

"Well, we figure whoever this guy is was pretty pissed off at Viv. Viv, for all intents and purposes, was this cute older lady who never harmed anyone. We come to learn she apparently gave away, again assuming, an illegitimate kid. Say this guy finds out that he was adopted. He goes looking for the woman who left him at the group home. What if, now it's a stretch, but what if…" Shuller dragged out the last of the sentence waiting for Susan to catch on.

"What? Are you suggesting that Levi is the kid Vivian dropped off at the group home? That's a bit much, don't you think? How the hell did you come up with that in the span of thirty-seconds?" Susan questioned.

Shuller shrugged.

"You need a vacation. You have no proof that he is in any way connected to her. You can't just start filling in blanks here. Levi had a decent life with the Swansons. What would make him snap to go and …" Susan stopped herself before the words *beat a woman to death with a bat* escaped her.

"Well, there were nine years of who knows what he went through as a kid. I'm pretty sure it was not the best childhood. Yeah, sure, he got a great family, eventually. But he could have repressed everything. Their untimely and unfair death may have triggered all that resentment and anger." Shuller was starting to convince himself.

"I'm just not sure how to prove he's the same kid."

"I'll go through the paperwork Vivian has in her files," Susan offered. "I don't recall seeing the name of the agency she worked with on the papers I found so far. Perhaps there is something with the name of the place she left him at still in those folders. If it's the same place, then it would be a bit easier for me to buy into your theory."

She saw Shuller nod in response to what she was saying, but he was still lost in his own thoughts.

"Proving he's the same kid does not instantly make him the murderer, you know that right?" Susan said, snapping him out of his daydream. "He's lived here a little while. If you resent your mother so much, why move to within feet of her house?"

"He was waiting. He learned her routine. He was finding the right time."

"Do you hear yourself? He bought a house and then sat and watched some woman's house just to learn her routine? She was practically a shut in, Martin. What routine?" Susan flipped her hands at Shuller.

"I don't know," he huffed out in frustration. "I just don't like this guy."

"That's apparent, but you can't pin a murder on him for that alone. You need to find a link. Why did he do it, motive, you know, basic police work?"

Shuller shot her a look.

"They may well be related, who knows. Hell, maybe that is why he did move here; he may have sought her out. But maybe, just maybe, he wanted to get to know her. Not kill her."

"He didn't try very hard to get to know her. His own words, 'I knew of her, but I didn't really know her. Never officially met her though.' How long did he live here and never tried to 'get to know her' if your scenario is true?" Shuller tossed the file folder onto his desk.

"He hasn't lived here that long. What did you want him to do? Ring her doorbell and say, '*Hi, I'm Levi, I just moved in around the block. I think you're my mom who dumped me thirty-some odd years ago. Up for some tea?*' " Susan said wide-eyed.

Shuller cocked his head and raised his eyebrows.

"Besides, I'm just assuming that is the reason he moved here. Just like you are assuming that he's guilty."

Shuller sighed heavily and hung his head. "You're right."

"More often than not, yes, yes I am," Susan smiled.

Shuller's desk phone rang, but before he had a chance to, Susan picked it up.

"Uh, huh. Yeah Danny, hold on. He's right here," she said as she extended the phone to him.

"Hey, Danny, what's up?" Shuller listened for a minute while Danny spoke. The lack of conversational cues irritated Susan a bit.

"Yeah, sounds good. I can just meet you over there. I should be fine, yeah. Don't worry about it. See you in a few minutes then," he said and hung up.

"I'm going out to meet up with Danny. He wants to check out something."

Levi was on edge ever since Danny left the garage. He could not shake the feeling that something may have tipped them off.

Did the cops have something? Did he leave behind a fingerprint or something? Levi was officially spooked.

One thought popped into his mind, the burn barrel. He never did check it after the fire went out to ensure that everything was gone. He found himself being preoccupied with getting home and checking it out. It was the longest day of his life.

As soon as it was time to leave, Levi was conscience enough to make it not look like he was too eager to get home. He was getting paranoid that the cops were watching. He tried to steady his nerves and go home at his normal speed without attracting too much, or any, attention, for that matter.

The issue he normally had to deal with during his ride home was no longer Vivian's house. He felt his stomach tighten as he passed the police station. He became aware that he was even sitting straighter, as if good posture was the way to throw them off the trail; a trail he was not quite sure they were even on just yet.

Levi got home and parked the 'Stang and got inside quickly. He closed the kitchen door behind him, turned and leaned his forehead against the closed door. It felt like he ran a marathon. He was breathing heavy and his heart was racing. Acting like it was a normal day had exhausted him. He threw his keys down on the table and made a beeline for the backyard.

Levi crossed over to the burn barrel and peered in. His heart sank to the pit of his stomach. There, staring back at him from within the burn barrel appeared to be a half burned pair of jeans and scraps of his boots. There was molten shoe sole up the side of the barrel.

Damn it! The fire should have been enough to get rid of everything, he thought.

Levi cursed himself for not checking that night to make sure if all went in the fire. He was too cocky that night. He was too full of himself that he got away with it that his arrogance stopped him from being certain. He knew that the cops really didn't have anything or else they would have him down at the station. He felt that too much time has passed since the murder. It was closing in. If they think him good for this, then they will start looking. They will find what's in the burn barrel.

Damn it, he screamed internally.

Levi looked around frantically for something else to burn legitimately. Just starting up a fire with nothing more than partially burnt jeans and boots would give off a god-awful smell. He only had the two palms and a small willow tree in his yard. He already took care of the debris from those the first time around. Levi panicked.

"I've got to find something else," he said. He knew that if there were not something else in that barrel to mask the smell of burning rubber, it would be obvious. He scanned the yard and saw a few half-dead Japanese boxwoods. *Perfect.* Levi darted over to the shed and grabbed his shovel. He set to work on pulling up the bushes. After a few jabs with the shovel and a little torque, the bushes came up easier than he thought.

PRODIGAL SON

He banged the dirt off them and used the shovel to break the bushes down to smaller portions in order to fit into the barrel. He stuffed the parts of one whole bush into the barrel. He crossed over to the fence and pulled off several vines of the yellow jasmine that was making its way across the back fence of the yard.

Maybe these will help with the smell, he thought as he dumped that in after the bush. He left the other bush he dug up close to the barrel in case it was needed. Levi ducked inside to grab a lighter. He snatched it from the counter and started back out to the yard. He got as far as the backslider when his chest tightened.

"You seem to be doing a number on this yard of yours. Those bushes could have been saved, you know." Shuller and Danny were leaning on the back fence.

"Couldn't help but notice you working out here, being over at Viv's checking out the backyard and all. Usually people wait until the weekend to rip apart the yard, not after a long day at work." Shuller stared at him coolly. He could not help but notice how Levi reacted to the two of them standing there. He had the "just caught with his hand in the cookie jar" look scrawled across his face. He just needed to get proof as to why he was apparently nervous around them.

"Well, I started this a while ago, and I was aiming to get the rest done and just never had," Levi said, trying to sound casual. "It's like you said, usually you do this on the weekend, but it's been a few weekends now and I just want to get this done already." He made his way toward the barrel. Again, he tried not to seem in too much of a hurry. He took two steps as Shuller stepped over the small fence.

"Well, I hate to interrupt your yard work," he said as he cleared the fence and stepped further into the yard, "but I just had something to clarify. If you don't mind?"

Levi felt as if he was going to pass out. Shuller was closing in on the burn barrel. He was certainly closer than Levi was and that alone unnerved him. Levi could not get to the barrel before Shuller. He would not be able to start the fire. He knew that if Shuller saw what was in the barrel, he'd certainly have a lot more questions.

Levi's mind started swirling with plan B's. He wanted to tell him he had no right on his property; he could just stay on the other side of the fence, but that would send up a flag he feared. He stood there and watched Shuller approach. The lack of response was all the permission he needed to stroll right up and figure it all out. Levi was so preoccupied with figuring a way out of this situation, it didn't register that Shuller was not only at the burn barrel, but pulling out the recently dug up bush and vines.

"See this wasn't so far gone. Just a little more attention was needed was all," Shuller said as he pulled the larger of the two portions from the barrel.

"Hey um, if you don't mind," Levi started to protest. He could not stop the way his voice broke at the exclamation.

"Problem, Levi?" Danny offered.

When did he come into the yard? Levi wondered. Danny stood a short distance behind Shuller.

Before Levi was able to respond to Danny, he watched wide eyed as Shuller leaned over the barrel and took a long look inside. He was helpless and lightheaded.

It's over.

Shuller's eyebrows rose. He turned his head to Danny and nodded for him to check out the barrel. Danny walked up, peered over, and smirked back to Shuller.

"So um, Levi, like I said, just wanted to clarify something here," Shuller said as he took a few steps toward Levi. He instinctively put his hand on the butt of his gun.

"Why exactly are you burning your jeans and work boots with such fervor?"

Levi felt all the air rush out of his lungs. Everything went quiet. It was a moment or two before he found his voice again.

"They were ruined, at work," he heard himself stutter.

"Then why not just throw them out? I mean, if they have some kind of motor oil or transmission fluid on them, it can't be good to burn them." Shuller wanted so bad to pounce on the guy. He took a slow and cautious step toward him. *Come on, you bastard.*

"Well, I wasn't sure if I could just toss them either, you know, environmentally speaking." Levi felt as if he was standing in quick sand. *He has nothing, right*, he thought. *Just some items in a burn barrel.* He could feel the sweat trickle down his temple.

"Don't you usually wear coveralls at the garage? Those are jeans in the barrel. Do you often work on cars without wearing coveralls?" Shuller was toying with him.

"Well, that's the thing, I wasn't at the time," he said. He was trying to justify why, but a plausible reason was not coming.

"I'm pretty sure the guys at the shop always wear coveralls, just so their own clothes don't get damaged," Shuller said looking at Levi through hooded eyes. "Isn't that like a shop policy?" Shuller knew he had him. He wanted to smack him around, just because he could.

While this exchange was going on between Shuller and Levi, Danny pulled out the remaining debris and broke off a branch. He started poking around in the barrel at the remnants. There seemed to be some sort of garbage bag around the edges of what seemed to be a pile of clothes partially remaining at the bottom of the barrel.

Whatever fire he had going before, it didn't get to the bottom of the barrel, Danny thought.

It seemed that Levi had apparently bunched or rolled his jeans up in some way before he pitched them into a bag, which he then tossed into the barrel. As Danny prodded at the remaining mass, it seemed that only the outer layer got scorched and burnt, but the interior contents, such as the jeans and boots, were only slightly licked by the fire. As to the jeans, it seemed that from the waist band to about the knee was still intact. This may prove problematic for Levi.

"Well, I'm no auto mechanic," Danny said as he came up behind Shuller, "but what's on the unburnt portion of those jeans, don't look like something you get spilled on you at the auto shop."

Shuller broke his glare at Levi long enough to see Danny give him a slow nod. Shuller knew he had him. He felt like as if he was going to burst into flames himself.

"Levi Swanson, you're under arrest for the suspicion of murder of Vivian Nash," Shuller said as he gripped his gun tightly. Danny moved around him, brought Levi's arms behind him, and started to cuff him. Levi just stared straight ahead in shock. He didn't have it in him to resist arrest. He didn't protest.

I was so close, he thought as his eyes left Shuller and drifted over to the barrel.

Shuller barely comprehended the Miranda Rights he heard Danny reciting to Levi. He let Danny take over and make the arrest at this point. Shuller kept his glare focused on Levi the whole time. It was all he could do to stay rooted to the ground. Danny speaking jolted him out of his thoughts.

"Boss? So I'll take him in, and you'll follow later?" Danny realized that Shuller was barely maintaining composure at this point.

"Yeah, yeah. Good. Thanks, Danny. I'll call this into the station. Get the boys out here for this," he said as he motioned over to the barrel. Shuller still had a firm grip on his gun the whole time he spoke.

Danny jerked Levi practically off his feet to get him to move. He led him past Shuller. For a moment, Danny was concerned that either would jump for the other as they neared each other, but they passed without incident. Danny had to pull Levi across the void and through Vivian's yard since they had parked in front of her house.

Shuller turned and watched for a minute. He watched as Danny pulled Levi across the grassy basin toward Vivian's house. He kept watching until they disappeared along the side of the house leading to the front yard. He wished he was the one bringing him in, but figured it was best. Given his relationship with the victim, he wanted a clean case against him. Shuller dug in his pocket for his cell phone. He pulled up his favorites and called the station.

"Suz? We're going to need forensics down at Levi Swanson's, on uh, Crescent View. Danny should be there soon with him, in fact. We got him."

KATHLEEN LOPEZ

Chapter Eleven

The sheriff's department had descended upon Levi's home within minutes of the arrest. Shuller stood back and watched the flurry of activities. He longed to get involved, but there was a nagging thought in the back of his mind. If Levi were the bastard Shuller had made him out to be, he'd be the type to get some scumbag lawyer that would use his involvement in the case as a reason to get it thrown out of court. That was the last thing Shuller wanted. He wanted this investigation to go off without a hitch. He wanted Levi brought down by the weight of what he had done alone. That meant for him to remain neutral, stand back, and not get involved in the exploration of Levi's house.

Shuller watched as the forensics team slowly pulled various charred items from the burn barrel, bagging them carefully. There were a few items already bagged up, such as the melted remains of Levi's work boots. The team was bagging up the most damning piece of evidence, Levi's jeans. From what Danny could scarcely see from that initial look into the barrel, those jeans seemed to be spattered with blood. The thought of it made Shuller turn his head involuntarily. He felt a strong urge to leave his post on the back patio to see what the team inside was discovering.

The officers inside found various bits of information that could lead to a possible motive for the killing. Inside the drawers of a desk, the team had found various papers from hospitals and registrars offices. Levi had apparently been investigating his own background.

"Anything good?" Shuller asked as he came up on one officer.

"It would seem Levi had obtained copies of his birth record and various papers regarding his adoption," the officer replied as he flipped through the documents.

"Anything with Vivian's name on it?" Shuller asked rather hopefully. He knew that there would not be an actual smoking gun hidden in that poor excuse of a desk. There would be nothing that screamed out showing a direct link between the two.

"Well, we did find some random notes and a file folder in there. Lots of docs from some state run facility for kids," he replied. "There is a form in there listing the mother as one Vivian Nash. It's not a hospital form, though. Odd, really. I don't think I've seen this type of record before."

Shuller wanted to leap for joy. He knew that would be enough, at least he'd hoped it would be. He stole a quick glance, peering over the arm of the officer to get a peek at the paper. It did look similar to the paperwork Vivian had in her files.

"Not sure why the kid was at an orphanage if she was the mom though, especially if it was Ms. Nash."

Shuller grimaced. He tried to put out of his mind the sense of trust he was violating when it came to this sorted mess. It was bad enough he was dealing with her gruesome murder, but digging into her life like this just compounded everything. He knew Susan was back at the office digging through her personal files, her life, trying to make sense of a hidden part of her life. Shuller felt as if there was still something not adding up. He was not sure if it was all the emotions this case brought to the surface or just an overwhelming sense of guilt for airing out her dirty laundry.

"You should probably vacate, boss."

Shuller turned to see Danny standing behind him. "Thought you were taking Levi in?"

"I was and did. Frank is processing him as we speak. When you didn't follow me back, I figured you were still here. If it is your intention to stay out of the way of this investigation, you seem to be doing a piss poor job, if I do say so myself."

"Okay, okay." Shuller chuckled. He threw up his hands in defeat. "I should probably head back to the station. I hear what you're saying."

"I'm sure Susan will have a better reign on you once you get there, so I have no worries that you'll be getting in the way," Danny said and smiled in earnest at the man.

"Brother, you have no idea." Shuller patted him on the shoulder and headed out the front door. He stopped and dropped his head back as if he was looking at the ceiling. He would have been if he hadn't screwed his eyes shut. He realized that they had parked in front of Vivian's house. It had seemed like hours ago they had first arrived. Perhaps it had been. Shuller seemed to have lost track of time once they had entered into Levi's backyard.

Shuller dropped his head back and headed out the backdoor. He didn't want to traverse that void behind the houses again, but the alternative of walking along the street seemed exhausting. When he entered into the backyard, the forensic guys were finishing up. It would seem they had emptied the barrel of its contents and had wrapped that in plastic, too. They wanted to make sure they grabbed everything they thought would help. Shuller smiled. He tried not to look at all the packages that lay on the ground. Try as he might, his eyes almost instantly fell to the bag containing the jeans. The way they were folded allowed Shuller to see just a bit of what Danny had seen that alerted him to the fact that Levi may have been destroying evidence. Shuller quickly darted his eyes forward and picked up his pace.

He needed to get out of there and fast. He hopped over the fence and suddenly didn't mind wading through the tall grass and weeds of the void. He wanted space between him and that house, those jeans. His mind kept that image in the forefront. No matter what he did, he could not shake it. Before he even realized it, he was at Vivian's back fence. He gripped the posts of the fence until his fingers turned white. He was out of breath, sweating. He didn't think he ran across the void, but it sure had felt like it. He closed his eyes and tried to get his breathing under control.

Danny had stepped out to check on the guys in the backyard when he caught sight of Shuller. He noticed him just standing on the outside of Vivian's fence. His head was slumped down and it would have seemed he was heaving. At first, Danny was not sure if he had broken down or was just out of breath, or even both. He stood there for a moment just watching the sheriff try to regain his composure. Just as he was about to head out to check on him, he saw Shuller lift his head. His breathing was no longer as noticeable from the distance.

Shuller took in one long deep breath and opened his eyes. He lifted his head and straightened his back. Of their own fruition, his gaze rose to the back window of Vivian's bedroom. He stared for a minute. He was not sure why he was just staring at her window. Was he expecting her to appear? Shuller's mind flashed to the day he and Danny ventured over to her house, the day he saw the room for himself. Shuller's grip on the fence never faltered.

Suddenly, Shuller felt the burn of bile in the back of his throat. He felt dizzy, nauseous. His chest tightened. His eyes rolled and his vision became dim and fuzzy. He tried to shake his head to clear away the feeling, but that seemed to make it worse. He felt as if he could not get in enough air. It was about that moment when he felt his knees give way.

"Shit!" Danny exclaimed as he darted for the back fence. His actions caught the attention of one of the forensic guys. Blindly, he followed Danny as he leapt over the fence and bolted for Vivian's house. Once they cleared the brush, the officer that became Danny's shadow found out why Danny ran toward the house.

Shuller was vaguely aware that he was on the flat of his back. He could not comprehend why the angle in which he was looking at Danny seemed odd to him. It took a few moments for the fog to lift and realize where he was. The garbled talk flowing from Danny also became clearer.

"Boss? Boss? You okay," Danny questioned. He was concerned since Shuller hadn't responded. It was if he didn't hear him. It sure looked to Danny that he didn't register him much at all. Then, he saw that the focus was slowly returning to his eyes. Shuller looked directly at Danny.

"What? Oh, yeah. I'm... uh, yeah," was all that Shuller muttered. He was just getting his bearings back. "Hey lend me a hand, huh?"

Danny and the officer flanked Shuller and both assisted the man to his feet. Shuller swayed upon standing up right for a moment, but then the feeling passed.

"You haven't answered me, at least not in a way that makes me feel comfortable yet. Are. You. Okay?" Danny searched the man's face waiting for an answer. He watched as the color was slowly returning from the ghastly pale white tone it was just moments before.

"Yeah. I'm fine, now. Just got the wind knocked out of me is all. No reason to be concerned." Shuller tried to wave off Danny's concern. It was not working.

"No reason to be concerned? Boss, you dropped like a stone."

The officer standing beside Shuller did his best not to engage or make eye contact. He caught Danny's attention and motioned with a nod of his head that he was going to head back to Levi's house. Danny nodded back to him then turned his attentions to Shuller.

Shuller glanced over his shoulder at the other officer's retreat. He cursed silently knowing this would make its way around the station. He didn't need the added interest by the guys when it came to this case.

"Be that as it may," Shuller started as soon as the other officer was out of hearing range, "I'm fine. I think it all just caught up with me or something. Seriously, Danny, I'm fine." Shuller felt the weight of Danny's gaze and tried to diminish it with a half-smile. Danny was not so easily deterred.

"How have you been dealing with all this?" Danny motioned with his hand at the two houses. "You haven't been saying much to me, but you been talking to Susan or Jeanie?"

"Jeanie is not part of the station," Shuller admonished him.

"Yeah, but she is a part of your life. We, on occasion, bring the job home with us, don't we? I think Jeanie would know not to run to the local press with anything you told her."

Shuller knew what he meant and instantly regretted his tone. Other than what little he and Susan had found out about Levi's childhood, he hadn't spoken to Jeanie too much about the case. It started to dawn on him that he hadn't really spoken much about it to anyone. Sure, he and Susan discussed theories, but not how it was affecting him directly.

"Boss? Kind of lost you there for a minute, again," Danny said, interrupting his thoughts.

"Ah, no. I haven't really talked to anyone about … this," Shuller said, nodding toward Vivian's house.

"Perhaps you should."

"What? Like a shrink? Not my kind of thing."

"You think all this is that bad that you'd need to see one?"

"Seriously, Danny, I'm fine. Alright, perhaps I haven't really been dealing with all this like I should."

"At the end of the day and all," Danny continued, "you're not really involved in the case, officially."

"Your point being?"

"My point is, if you talked to Jeanie, you're not putting anything at risk. I mean you're aware of the finer points, but like I said earlier. I don't think she'll run to the papers. It may be good to just talk out what's going on in your head, just to get it out."

Shuller started to consider what Danny was telling him. He began to wonder if he should talk to Jeanie. He's already shared with her some items discovered about Levi, but that was not even part of the investigation. Perhaps it would be since he'd been arrested, but it didn't change the fact that she already knew them.

Shuller was so lost in his thoughts that he nearly forgot Danny standing there. The implied question still hung heavy between the men.

"You're right. I should just get it out. I'd hate to dump all that on Jeanie. I mean, I'm still new at all this with her. That seems like a lot of heavy crap to burden someone with."

"I think she can take it. She already puts up with you; what's a little more?" Danny questioned lightheartedly.

"Nice."

"Why don't you knock off for the day? Call Jeanie, order in." Danny's suggestion began to sound more inviting the more purchase Shuller lent it.

"Sounds good." Shuller's surprise at giving in was matched by Danny. Even he was shocked at how easy it was to pack it in for the day. The whole situation must have been weighing on him more than he realized to, by his own standards, shirk responsibility and leave early for the day.

Danny took a step back as Shuller crossed over the small back fence. He took note how Shuller seemed to try to avoid looking toward the house. He was not sure if that was a good sign or not. Shuller trudged up the yard and alongside the house. Danny watched until he was out of view.

PRODIGAL SON

Shuller made his way down the alleyway between the two houses until he reached the front yard. He barely trusted a look back but thought better not to try. He kept a steady pace as he kept his car in his sights before him. His head was clearer than it was moments ago. He still felt off, but felt okay to drive. He considered calling Jeanie, but then decided to just head straight over to the firehouse instead.

It became the single most thought to him, getting to Jeanie. Whether he was really okay to drive or not, he had to get to that station house. Everything would be fine once he got there, he convinced himself. He found himself in autopilot once behind the wheel. Again, whether or not that was a safe mode to be in while in a moving automobile he was unsure. It only took a few moments to get to the firehouse, to Jeanie. It was as if the whole trip was one blur as he put the car in park. He knew that to be problematic.

Jeanie.

The idea was becoming more precious than air. He was not sure why the desire merely to see her was so strong. He had to will himself out of the car. The heft of his own body was fighting him. His legs were suddenly laden down with lead. The few feet it was from the car to the station house doors felt as if Shuller was slogging through the thickest mud. He was now getting to that concerned place Danny was just minutes ago.

What the hell is happening? he wondered. He had been fine all this time. *Why now?* They were so close to having it all over and done with at this point.

Off in what seemed the far distance, Shuller heard someone call out to him. It was the faintest of whispers to him. He squinted to concentrate to hear where it was coming from. He felt as if it was coming from his left. As he turned, he saw two firemen coming out of the bay door. They appeared to be saying something. Shuller could make out that their mouths were moving but figured the wind was pulling the sound with it. It was then Shuller saw past them to the trees that lined the back of the lot. They stood tall, steady. No wind. His attention shifted back to the two firemen who approached him.

They still attempted to speak, but Shuller could not comprehend what they were trying to say. Then he noticed something odd. As they got closer to him, they became more and more out of focus. Shuller rubbed his eyes to clear out whatever cobwebs obscured his vision. It didn't work. They were close enough to hear sounds, but still to Shuller, it was garbled noise. He suddenly felt queasy. His mouth felt pasty; his head swam and felt heavy. The last thing he registered was the two firemen were running toward him just as everything faded.

He heard the steady whoosh of a fan; felt the cool breeze sweep across his face. There was a creaking, no, more of a soft crunch of a leather cushion he heard and then realized he felt. He realized there was a cool terry cloth on his forehead, getting cooler from the breeze of the overhead fan. Disembodied voices were all around him. He laid and waited, listening.

"We tried to get over to him before he hit," one voice said. "He swayed a bit and then his legs just gave out beneath him."

"It's probably the case," another voice said. It was the way they said *the case* that struck him as if it was hard to ignore the spotted elephant dancing before them in the bright pink taffeta tutu.

"Looks as if he's coming around," yet another voice said as Shuller cracked open an eye. The harshness of the overhead florescent lights almost burned his eyes. Squinting through hooded eyes, he started to take into account where he was. It appeared to be the firehouse chief's office.

"Whoa there, Sheriff. Not so fast," said the house medic as he pushed a still disoriented Shuller back down on the couch. "You're not quite ready to get up just yet."

"What happened?" Shuller said easing back down on what he realized was the worn leather couch in the chief's office. He felt as if he was nursing the mother of all hangovers.

"Well, the short of it, you collapsed on the street outside the firehouse. Our boys tried to get to you, but you managed to beat them to the pavement first. You got yourself a nice knot here on your head."

Shuller reached around and found the spot the medic mentioned. As soon as his hand came in contact, he jerked it away as if he burnt his hand. A soft and gentle hand then encompassed his.

"Shh. There," Jeanie said. She was crouched by the sofa holding Shuller's hand in one hand while the other combed through his hair.

"Relax. This is going to be a bit cold," she said as she eased an ice pack to the side of his head.

Shuller flinched a bit, not from the cold, but the pressure. He could not miss the concern in her voice. He was rather concerned himself.

"Should he go and get checked out?" she asked of the medic.

"I'm fine. I just need to get some rest, a break from work," Shuller said. He was startled how hoarse and broken his voice sounded aloud.

"Shh. No really, should I bring him to the hospital?"

Shuller was taken aback at her dismissal, even more so at the swat to his arm he received for interrupting. Jeanie was not taking anything from him now.

"He doesn't seem to be concussed. Going home and getting rest? Yes, that seems to be in high order here."

"Okay. Chief? Alright if I take him home?"

"And face you if I say no? Heck, you just smacked the man, and he's injured. I'm not taking you on, not now," Chief chuckled. "Looks like we both have our crosses to bear with strong-willed women in the office, huh Sheriff."

"You have no idea," Shuller said as his eyes rolled shut. He started to think what Susan was going to say once she heard about this incident.

"Hell, you got it coming and going," he said laughing, that is until Jeanie shot him a look.

"Ah-hum, yes, we'll give him a minute or two to get his bearings, then feel free to help him to his place, Jeanie," Chief said, a bit abashed. "Let's give him some air, boys. Take as much time as you need, Sheriff."

The chief motioned to the small crowd in his office to start filtering out. Shuller felt embarrassed. He kept his eyes closed as to avoid seeing the look of pity on the firemen's faces. He was not sure why they would, but from the bits of conversation he picked up on as he was coming around, it sounded as if they were figuring that the case was getting the better of him. He was not so sure they were wrong, either. As he heard the office door click closed, he tilted his head toward Jeanie and looked at her through his lashes. What he saw was concern with an undercurrent of angry girlfriend.

"Are you alright?"

"I'm fine. Yeah."

"Seriously? Don't bullshit me. Fine people don't drop out in the street. What's going on?"

"Honestly?"

"That would be nice," she said, cutting him off. And there it was; concern was losing the battle against angry girlfriend.

"Honestly, I'm not sure."

"We'll start at the beginning. What happened today? Has this been happening before or is this new?"

Concern is trying to make a comeback against angry girlfriend.

"No. It hasn't happened before today. I was over at Vivian's. Danny called me over to try to get a different set of eyes on the point of entry. While we were out on the back porch, we caught sight of Levi Swanson out in his backyard. He was frantically trying to burn something in a barrel out back." Shuller started to whisper.

"So he was burning something in a barrel. That's what you do with a *burn* barrel, Marty."

"No, it was more than that. He was driven. In a frenzy. That's what caught our attention. We crossed over to him and...," Shuller paused. He rolled over more to face her directly. Jeanie moved in a bit.

"We got him."

Jeanie took a second to understand what he was saying.

"Wait. What?" she said as her eyes went wide.

"Turns out he was trying to burn *evidence*," Shuller cautiously croaked out. He started to worry if he should say just what. He thought he'd dance around the topic for a minute or so before he started divulging investigation information.

"Wow," Jeanie whispered loudly. "Stuff linking him to the case? Wait, can you tell me this kind of stuff?"

"Well, something potentially linking him, let's go with that. Something that seems to be damning evidence. Certainly not what you'd normally burn in a barrel. We had interrupted him before he had a chance to eliminate it. Danny arrested him, and we got the boys out there to tag and bag."

"That's fantastic! So wait. What does this have to do with you collapsing outside?"

"That's where this all gets fuzzy, no pun intended. I hung back a bit while the guys were there when Danny came back from the station. We talked how I should take off. I walked back toward Vivian's when I felt dizzy."

"This wasn't your first blackout? You need to tell that to the medic. Better yet, you need to go to the hospital," Jeanie frantically gestured as she spoke.

"Calm down, Jeanie. I didn't black out, just dropped out, a bit."

Even Shuller was not buying that line of bull. Jeanie confirmed that she was not buying it either.

"So whatever this is, it's escalating. I see. No cause for alarm there."

Ding, ding, ding. We have a winner. Angry girlfriend for the TKO.

"I don't think I did myself any favors by driving over here right after that."

"Danny let you drive?"

"Like I said, it wasn't as bad as what just happened. Danny thinks that I've been stressed out and I think that is probably what this is. I haven't tried to deal with all of this, and maybe it has affected me more that I realized."

Shuller felt the impact of those words more since they are coming directly from him. Jeanie's expression softened a little.

"After her death, I didn't really stop and take into account how it affected me. I don't know. I mean, we weren't related, but kind of felt like it after a while, you know. Then when Suzie Q and I found out that she held this massive secret from me. A kid? That's huge. It totally changed how I saw her. But I couldn't talk to her about it. I couldn't ask why. Hell, I was not even sure if it was my place to ask why. Again, we weren't related so it was not my business. But if she and her life weren't my business, then why leave everything to me? It would have seemed from the outside that I meant more than just the local law officer guy."

Shuller sighed heavily. He rolled back and stared at the ceiling.

"So," Jeanie started playing armchair therapist. "Now that it seems all buttoned up and done, you think your mind decided to suddenly allow you to take it all in? Like it's okay now since there is a foreseeable conclusion?"

"Maybe. I'm not sure. All I know is it feels as if I ran a marathon with a small elephant on my back, and my head is killing me."

"Don't know about the elephant part, but head-butting the concrete may have something to do with that headache."

"Humor? Really?" Shuller shot her a sideways glance. He gave her a meek smile. She returned a similar smile back.

"Do you think you can try sitting up? Don't fall on me. I don't think I can manage getting you up off the floor myself."

"I think I can manage."

Shuller slowly swung his legs off the arm of the couch and planted his feet onto the floor as he slowly rose to a sitting position. He swallowed and took a deep breath. He was waiting if the swaying feeling was going to return. It seemed to be kept at bay.

"So far, so good."

Jeanie still looked on with concern. She waited a few moments to ensure he really did have his barring before she suggested he move more.

"I'll get my things then. I can move the car around maybe?"

PRODIGAL SON

"I can make it to the car, Jeanie," Shuller said with the hint of unintentional annoyance. He gave a slight nod to her as an offering of apology. Jeanie seemed to accept the notion and continued gathering her things.

Jeanie slung her purse over her shoulder and crossed back over to Shuller. She helped the man to his feet and held him steady. Shuller let out a soft chuckle.

"I'm not going to fall over," he assured her.

"Are you sure?"

"Yeah, eighty-nine percent sure."

"That's reassuring," she smirked as they started out of the office. The firehouse seemed scarce of firefighters as they walked from the bay. The guys had apparently given them a wide berth and found elsewhere to be. As they walked into the parking lot, the sun appeared amplified to the extent that Shuller had to squint just to see initially. Jeanie hovered but not too closely. Her arm rested around his waist with the faintest tension. If he wobbled slightly, Shuller felt her grip tighten. He realized they were headed to her car.

"I'll let Danny know where my car is," he said, realizing it was a squad car and not his personal car that he had taken to Vivian's house.

"*I'll* call Danny later," she admonished. "You are coming home to rest. I'll worry about the little stuff."

"Yes, ma'am."

Shuller eased into the car and rested his head back against the seat. He felt more than heard the car door close beside him. As he lifted his head to look at the door, the driver's side opened and Jeanie dropped into her seat.

"Good to go?" she asked as she closed the door with one hand and put the key in the ignition with the other.

"All good here, boss." He smiled.

"That's right, boss. Don't you forget that now."

They shared a chuckle as Jeanie pulled out of the parking lot and started out for his house.

Levi sat. He stared straight ahead. He was motionless, expressionless, and basically unresponsive. Try as he might, Danny could not break through. He tried getting himself directly in Levi's eye line, but that had little effect. Danny figured this was either some tactic, a basis for an insanity defense, or the bastard was in some sort of shock. If it was the latter, he didn't care. He needed him to talk, lie, confess, something. Danny was doing all he could not the blow up at the guy. Levi was making that nearly impossible.

"Do you want to tell me about how you really do know Vivian Nash?"

"Don't you mean did?" The first thing Levi said in almost an hour, and it was that.

Danny thought that was going to send him over the top. He took in a deep breath and swallowed. He plastered on a tight smile and continued.

"Yes. How did you know Vivian Nash?"

Levi's eye dropped the glazed look and refocused onto Danny. "I didn't."

"You didn't know her?"

Levi shook his head.

"You killed someone you didn't know?"

Levi nodded his head. Danny was astounded. While they had video rolling, he wanted him to say it. He needed a full on confession. He needed this not so much for Vivian, but for Shuller as well.

"You killed Vivian Nash? I need a verbal answer here. Tell me you understand what I'm…"

"I killed her," Levi said, cutting Danny off cold. Danny thought he could not be more shocked than he was a moment ago. He could not have been more wrong.

"Okay, the million dollar question. Why? Why did you kill Vivian Nash?"

Levi took a moment, as if he was collecting his thoughts. It was a painstakingly slow process.

"I killed her *because* I didn't know her."

Danny thought he was the one who was insane. He stared at Levi, who again, remained emotionless. He could not understand the rationale behind what he just heard. Levi finally decided he was going to elaborate.

"She was a stranger. Do you believe that? A stranger to me. That should not have been the case, you'd think anyway. I never knew her."

This was getting stranger and stranger for Danny. He was not sure what Levi's deal was, but he knew he was missing a piece of the puzzle. He was just hoping that Levi's egg was not cracked and was actually lucid enough to fill in the gaps.

"I'm missing something here, Levi. I get you didn't know her. That seems to be the issue here. Why is that the issue? Were you *supposed* to know her? Why?"

"Of course I was supposed to know her!" he screamed and practically bolted upright from the chair.

Danny was never more thankful for the secured handcuffs tethering him to the table.

"Who does that to a kid? Just leaves them, throws them out like they were trash. She just left me, you know? Just left me there at that hellhole of a place. Hell, she left me there so I would be someone else's problem. She didn't give a damn about me. I was a problem to get rid of. She didn't care what would happen to me. If she'd only knew. God. If she knew what some of those foster houses were like, how they treated me. But who am I kidding? She didn't even think twice about me after that day, the heartless bitch."

Danny was struck silent. He was trying to process the sweet lady with Levi's description of her. It was not meshing with the picture in his head.

"After my parents died, I found that home again. That group home. That excuse of a childhood I had. I went there to find out why. Why someone would leave me. I just lost the only people I could call my parents. I just wanted that again. I wanted to know who my parents were; the ones who left me. I wanted to find them and ask them why. I traveled to that group home and met with the person who ran it. It was not that crooked old bitch that used to run it. It was some pencil pushing idiot. He told me he couldn't give me my files. Do you believe that? *My* files. I couldn't see them. He actually had the nerve to show me where they were in the filing cabinet before shutting the drawer. Seriously?" Levi shook his head.

"Then some snot nosed bastard had some problem and he was called out of the office. So as soon as he left, I snatched the folder and took off. That's where I saw the papers. How she brought me there when I was a baby. I was only a few days old. She dropped me off like I was the dry cleaning."

"Alright. Let me get this straight. Vivian Nash was your mother. She gave you up for adoption, so you tracked her down some thirty years later and beat her to death with a baseball bat?"

Danny sat wide eyed at the mechanic sitting across from him in interrogation. The rationale was there, at least for Levi, not for any other particularly sane individual.

Levi stared back at the detective. The idea wasn't repugnant or unfathomable. It made perfect sense to him. With that in mind, he answered Danny's question.

"Basically, yes."

Levi huffed. He was tired of talking about her. He felt as if he said it a million times. *If he wants to hear it then fine*, he thought. He leaned in across the table and took a deep breath. He stared Danny dead in the eye before he spat out what Danny was so desperate to hear.

"I killed Vivian Nash. She left me in that dump as a kid because she could not be bothered, the rich bitch. And I'll tell you what else. I don't regret not one fucking swing of that bat!"

Shuller woke up groggily from his nap. The room was considerably darker than it was when they first got home. He was in his bed, clothed, on top of the sheets. He barely remembered making it home. It started to come back to him in drips and drabs. Jeanie drove up to his townhouse and parked in the driveway. She took the keys from him and opened the door, and before he had the chance to protest even, Jeanie took hold of him around the waist as she had before and led him to the stairs. He was going to lie down in his bed come hell or high water.

He remembered making it to the bed. Jeanie had handed some pills to him and a glass of water. He took them without even asking as the feeling of exhaustion started to take a hold of him again. He settled back into the bed and vaguely remembered Jeanie talking to him as he started to drift off. Shuller started to realize that he might have even drifted off as she was talking to him.

He laid there for a moment or two. He then heard Jeanie downstairs in the kitchen. It had sounded like she was talking, perhaps on the phone. Phone. Shuller reached for his in his pocket, but it wasn't there. He turned his head to the nightstand and it wasn't their either. Shuller chuckled. She must have fished it out of his pocket he assumed. The tone of her voice gave him a pang of concern. Despite the hell he may catch for leaving his bed, he had to go and check on Jeanie.

"Wow, just wow. I don't have much more for you there, Danny. Yeah, well he's upstairs sleeping. Better, much better. Doc said I could give him some aspirin and have him lie down to recoup. I think it just all hit him like a ton of bricks once it was all coming to an end. Humph." Jeanie said as she turned at the sound of Shuller making his way down the stairs. "Well he *was* sleeping, but here he comes now," she said with a grimace directed at Shuller.

Shuller shrugged a little at her and mouthed Danny as he motioned for the phone. She nodded her head back at him.

"Okay, well here he is. You get him revved up, and you and I will have words," she warned him before handing over the phone.

Shuller took the phone. He already had a feeling something unexpected happened with the case given the tone and facial expressions he was getting from Jeanie. Jeanie came around behind Shuller and led him to the chair she pulled out by his dinette. She guided him down and took the chair next to him.

"Hey, Danny. I'm fine, or will be. Yeah, yeah. Stress or something," he was saying in response to Danny asking about his latest spill.

"So, what's going on? Nothing bad I hope."

"Boss, it's the damnedest thing," Danny said. "He confessed. No fuss, no muss. Just up and came out with it."

"You're kidding?" Shuller could not believe it himself. Jeanie raised her eyebrows and nodded her head at what she assumed Danny just told him.

"I have it on tape. I made sure he said it seven ways to Sunday. He never once denied it, tried to talk around it, or nothing. Bastard just rolled out with it."

"What the hell was his reason?" Shuller sat dumbfounded.

"Apparently, this little grease monkey didn't get enough hugs from Mommy," Danny quipped. "He tells me this tale, how he was pissed off at Vivian for giving him up, putting him in foster care and all. Apparently, either the place was a hellhole, or the foster families were. Probably a combination of both. Anyway, he harbored this resentment for her all these years."

"Did you talk to Suzie Q? We had dug up some info on this childhood."

"Yep. She brought that to my attention once we had him in booking. Also, the lab guys say that were tagging paperwork that Levi had on his computer and in his desk. Apparently," Danny said as he shuffled some pages in the file folder he was holding before continuing, "he had obtained some files from the group home about being left at the orphanage. He used this and some other tidbits of info here and there to find her. I guess after his adopted parents died, something snapped for him."

Shuller was shocked it was that easy. There has to be another shoe fall. Nothing closes that neatly.

"We have everything, right? I mean, kind of anti-climactic if you ask me." That received a swat to the arm from Jeanie.

"You've got to admit, it's too easy; too quick," he whispered to her as he covered the phone. She shrugged a bit in response.

"He's a nut, boss. Boys are processing him now. He signed a confession. Oh, and before you ask, we are having him evaluated in case he claims some temporary insanity plea. But given all the paperwork at the house, the forethought to burn the evidence, I don't think that is a possibility."

PRODIGAL SON

"Okay, well great, then, uh…" Shuller was at a loss.

"I know how you feel, boss. I was there and I don't believe it myself. Well, I should get back to it and make sure we have all our T's crossed and our I's dotted on this one."

"Sure thing. I'll be here," Shuller said and hung up.

He gaped at Jeanie. He was at a loss for what to say or do.

"I know, right? What the hell?" was all she could muster.

"Do you want some tea?" Jeanie needed something to do while it all sunk in herself.

Shuller smiled. "Well, it *is* evening."

Shuller strode into the office without letting the boys know he was coming back. Frank, again, was shocked to see him in.

"Well, boss, you look rested," he said cheerily.

Shuller, on the advice of the medic and Jeanie's watchful eye, had taken a week off. The rest, combined with the close of the Vivian Nash case did him wonders.

"I feel much better."

It was the understatement of the year. The rest of the boys started to notice Shuller's presence and slowly said their hellos as he came around the desk and headed to his office.

"So, I see the warden let you out," Susan joked.

"Yeah. She felt I was okay to rejoin society. Odd week, huh?"

"Um, a bit."

She followed Shuller into his office. Despite his unannounced appearance, Susan was already prepared to give him a rundown of what happed while he was on leave. Jeanie was good to hide his phone and limit stressors for him while he took off.

"Well, Levi has got a fight on his hands, or at least his lawyer. They booked him on first-degree murder, which has the lovely added benefit to normal and sane people of the death penalty. His lawyer is trying to get that off the table, but good luck there. He is aiming for life without parole. I'd rather prefer the first option where I don't have my tax dollars paying for him, but in the end, either works for me."

"Well, don't hold back, Suzie Q. Tell me what you really think."

"Other than that craziness, we've all been pretty good while you were resting. Oh, there is one thing that needs your attention though."

"Oh?" Shuller was sort of itching for work to do. Resting at home was nice, even more so with Jeanie there, but he wanted to get back to work.

"Yeah. Davie needs help with his stance a bit. He's been missing the curve balls and was hoping you'd help him out."

"Not a problem." Shuller laughed. "We can work on that for certain. Is there anything else pressing?"

"No, that was the big one. I have to go and consolidate all that paperwork we collected about Levi for the prosecutor's office. I need to jump on that. Files for your review in your inbox," Susan said as she left his office.

Shuller sat in his chair and listened. He heard the comforting sounds of the normal scene once again. Phones ringing, water cooler conversations in the distance, and the typical office commotion. It was just like it was when he got back from Columbus Cove. Still, something was amiss. He could not put his finger on it, but there was something waiting. He was thrilled Vivian's case closed so easily for them, but something unsettling was still waiting. He could feel it. He wasn't sure what, but he knew it was there. Life wasn't always so neat and clean.

Shuller had a nagging feeling in the back of his mind that the penny has yet to drop.

KATHLEEN LOPEZ

Epilogue

Susan could not believe what she was seeing. The files were spread across the conference room table. She scrambled from one stack to the other.

"This can't be right," she questioned. She scanned one document furiously before flipping to another. Her brow furrowed as she read over the contents of the documents.

"This would mean..." she started, but stopped at the mere thought of what she was about to say.

"No. No, this isn't, *is it?* I've got to find Martin."

No, wait, she thought. *Let me make sure one more time.*

Susan was trying to go through all the documents and notepads she and Shuller collected while investigating Levi's past. She had all the group home papers, the adoption papers, but the dates were off. It was an oversight on their parts, but they were not meeting up.

Susan reviewed the papers from the group home. What they had from their investigation seemed to be what Levi had also obtained. So she knew she was working from the same information Levi was, but those dates.

The date from Levi's hospital records were way off from what was listed for the group home of his arrival. There was a year gap.

That was no way a typo, she thought. She was studying the paperwork when Danny stepped into the conference room

"Couldn't help but notice you seem to be having some difficulties, Suz. Anything I can help you with?"

"Yeah, close the door, would you?" she whispered. "Now come here."

Danny quickly moved to the door and closed it before rounding the table.

"These papers are from the group home. They say that Levi arrived at the group home on March 23, 1978; 36 years ago. Now here is a birth record for a child dropped off at the home, dated March 23, 1977."

"What?" Danny took the papers from Susan's hands and toggle back and forth between the two.

"That can't be right. How could they say he arrived in 1978, but Levi's hospital records show he was born a year earlier?"

"These aren't the same kids. All the paperwork in this one folder is for two separate kids. We assumed that Vivian brought Levi to the group home a few days after he was born, but in digging through what I have here, the timelines don't make sense if you think this all belongs to one kid. There is a birth record here from a midwife *and* a hospital record of a birth. There would be no reason for two birth records like this. In Vivian's files, I found research she did for a midwife service. Vivian, indeed, did use a midwife to deliver her child. Those birth records belong to her child. Levi has a hospital issued birth record. That would mean that Levi was not Vivian's child."

"You've got to be kidding me? Wait, what does this mean for the case? We based his motive on the fact that he was left at this group home and built up this resentment for her. Now it turns out that wasn't even him! He admitted killing her. What does this do for the case?"

"Easy there. You're forgetting one thing. He assumed the same damn thing," Susan reminded him. "He based his reasoning on killing Vivian for leaving him at that hellhole, but he missed the fact that the years were different on the birth records, or that there were two of them. I guess he was so enraged and grief stricken at that point to even notice. I almost didn't catch it either until I was trying to correlate this mess for the prosecutor. The records that Levi took from the group home are crap. It is easy to see why they were mixed up. Both kids were both born on March 23. However, some idiot just read March 23, figured it was the same kid, and didn't bother to make sure the years matched before they were filed together. Great record keeping. We have two lives here all twisted together. Oh, my God," Susan stopped.

"What? What is it?"

"It just hit me. He killed her for no damn reason! I haven't come across why he was there, but it wasn't the story he built up. I know you just said that, but it literally is just sinking in. Not sure what the deal was there, but doesn't seem as dramatic as he played it up in his head."

Danny started scrounging around through the file folders that Susan hadn't finished correlating yet. Danny flipped furiously and found what he was looking for.

"Oh God, get this. It would seem there was an accident, looks like a car accident. These must be Levi's parents since the dates work. Man, how ironic. Just like his adoptive parents. Jesus! He wasn't abandoned. His parents were killed in the wreck, and he survived with injuries. He had no other family so once he was released from the hospital; the state placed him at the home when he was barely a few months old!"

"Oh my God. Viv was killed for no reason. That makes it all more tragic, if that was even possible." Susan's face fell. She then inhaled sharply. "Martin just got back today. How do we tell him this?"

"Just leave that to me. I'll figure it out." Danny seemed to get lost in thought for the moment. "Funny though," Danny trailed off.

"What on Earth could be funny about any of this?"

"Well maybe funny is the wrong word, but March 23, 1977. Isn't that Shuller's birthday?"

"Oh, wow, yeah. What are the odds?"

"Oh, it gets stranger than that. Shuller was adopted. Did you know that?"

"What? No, he wasn't!"

"Yep. We were catching a game once at his place and his sister called about coming out to see him with the kids and stuff, pretty normal. After he got off the phone, I asked if they were close. It kinda seemed a bit strained over the phone. He tells me that they were, *considering*."

"Considering?"

"Exactly what I ask him. Then he tells me that he was adopted. He doesn't talk about it much 'cause he says it doesn't matter in the end really, or at least itshould not. The family is close and all, but he said he knew early on, and it always stuck in the back of his mind. Equal, but separate, or something like that."

"Did he ever say anything about his real family?"

"Nope. Says he never knew them and was fine with that. Honestly, he is. No ill will like some people we know. Funny though. Same date."

"Uh, Danny," Susan felt a knot in the pit of her stomach.

"What's the matter?"

"This group home is in New York."

"Yeah, so?"

"So is Martin's family. Do you think ... I mean, like you said, what are the odds?"

"Wait. Are you thinking he came from the same group home? That would mean...are you saying that you think Shuller is the baby that was dropped off? Oh, come on. Now that's stretching it a bit, don't you think?"

"That's exactly what I'm saying. Vivian dropped off a baby at the home. Same date, practically, you said it yourself!"

Susan's mind raced. She started reviewing all the information she had in her head.

"Okay, hear me out. Vivian and Richard lived in New York when he was shipped overseas for the military. She stayed there until he returned. Upon his retirement, the family home, her house here in town, was transferred over to them. They lived in New York during that time. We already figured that Vivian had an affair and that the baby wasn't her husband's, so she had to get rid of it."

"These are all assumptions, Suz. It's not like we can ask or verify anything here."

"But think about it. It connects. All the dots connect. Martin's adopted, in New York. He was born on March 23, 1977. Vivian gave up a kid, in New York, born on March 23, 1977."

Danny started connecting all the dots. Susan's logic made sense.

"Wait, wait. Shuller *is* Vivian's kid? Is that what we're saying here? Seriously?"

"Martin was always baffled why her estate was left to him in her will. Guess what I found? In the other file folders we have, I found some files that she contacted a private investigator. She must have had him followed or something; trying to find out how he was. There were several bills over the years for the same agency. Periodically, she would contact them and have them, I don't know, check up on him. Then there's the copy of her will, redone of course after Richard died, that's when she left everything to Martin. They've known each other for years and Martin never knew!"

"Okay, say this all is true, which I have a hard time believing, but at the same time I must admit, it is clicking into place. Vivian had a family home out here. Shuller's family is from New York. How do you explain that Shuller just happened to move to the same small town she happened to live in?"

"Vivian's family had money. Old money. Not sure from where or what, but they did. Vivian had a college grant established. Shuller *just happened* to get it? Not suspicious at all, right?. She got him to come out to college, here, in Arizona."

"Okay, so Vivian has a kid, drops him off at an orphanage to hide him from the husband, tracks him his whole life, practically stalks him for years and then engineers it so they wind up in the same small town? That's what you're saying? Sounds too far-fetched to me!"

"Yep. Point out where I'm wrong, go ahead."

Danny looked at all the paperwork again. He would read one page then the next and shake his head.

"Well?"

"I'm looking, woman, give me a minute here."

"You can't rebuke it. It all maps out."

"That's crazy."

"As crazy as killing a woman on the idea she's your long lost mother, but oops, turns out not exactly? Isn't this the craziest thing you ever heard? Think about it. Vivian wasn't Levi's mother, she was Martin's. Now I ask you, how are you going to tell him that?" Susan looked at Danny knowing there was no easy answer.

"I don't have a friggin' clue! I don't know, Suz. It maps out, I'll give you that. But where's the smoking gun? Where is that one piece that cements the case here? Show me that, and I'll tell the man myself. Where in this trunk is that one piece that ties the two of them together, that proves everything you just said?"

Shuller stood behind the closed door to the conference room. The door was surprisingly thin, as he just realized. He wanted to lend a hand to Susan when he heard the two of them talking. When he heard his name brought up in conversation, his hand stopped short of opening the door and hovered over the doorknob. He froze when he picked up on the subject matter.

He listened to Susan's string of logic, the back and forth of the two of them. He was reeling. He could not find fault in anything she said. While on paper it could match up, Shuller's mind turned to harder facts.

Couldn't be, he thought. Then it struck him, what Danny said. He realized that Susan didn't have all the contents from the trunk. The box. That first box he brought into his office the day he found out about Vivian's secret. Shuller darted back to his office. He quickly entered and shut the door behind him. He scanned the room until he locked eyes on that box. He clicked the door lock and collected the box. He placed it on the table in front of the couch and stared at it.

"This is ridiculous," he said to the empty room. "It's probably more junk collected by a lonely lady."

Shuller took a deep breath and opened the box. There were no files, just random items. He saw a lace lined linen handkerchief lying on top of what seemed to be a shawl. Shuller started to pull the items from the box. He let out a breath he didn't realize he was holding. The box, as he suspected, had random knick-knacks in it, nothing that was Danny's smoking gun. A pair of gloves and a wool cap later, Shuller got to the bottom of the box.

There was a tattered old scrapbook. A smile crept across Shuller's face. He assumed that she had some old pictures of her and

PRODIGAL SON

Richard. He took the book and sat on the couch. Opening the book without a second thought, the smile on Shuller's face vanished as quickly as it appeared. Staring back at him from the pages of the scrapbook was...him.

It was a newspaper clipping from a local paper. Shuller had received some citizen's award when he was in grade school for helping with a nursing home as a part of his Boy Scout troop.

What on Earth? he mused.

He could not believe what he was seeing. He flipped the page and there was a picture of him and his grade school friends in the courtyard. There were random pictures of him, articles from the local paper of his football prowess, and some notes scribbled on a slip of paper, apparently from the PI she had hired.

There it was, Danny's smoking gun, sitting in his lap. Vivian had a record of his school life, his school pictures, and his childhood in snapshots, in the pages of a scrapbook.

Her DNA's on file, he suddenly thought. *The lab guys could run it against mine, just to make sure. Oh, my god, is this really true?*

It would explain the strange need to check in on her, why she left him everything, how he felt about her. Was that the concern of a son for his aging mother? It would certainly explain why she had a scrapbook of his life staring back at him. It would have seemed the penny had dropped for Shuller.

Made in the USA
Columbia, SC
12 May 2021